DADDY WOLF'S LITTLE STAR
SILVER WOLF SHIFTERS BOOK 3

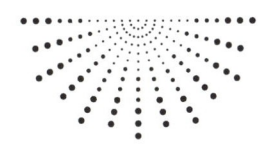

BE KELLY

Daddy Wolf's Little Star (Silver Wolf Shifters Book 3)

Copyright © 2020 by BE Kelly.

Cover design: Michelle Sewell- RLS Images Graphics and Designs

Imprint:Independently published

First Print Edition: October 2020

All rights reserved.

No part of this book may be reproduced, scanned, or distributed in any printed or electronic form without permission. Please do not participate in or encourage piracy of copyrighted materials in violation of the author's rights. Thank you for respecting the hard work of this author.

This is a work of fiction. Names, characters, places, and incidents either are the product of the author's imagination or are used fictitiously, and any resemblance to locales, events, business establishments, or actual persons— living or dead—is entirely coincidental.

PROLOGUE

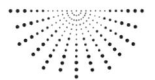

Lake

Ten years earlier:

LAKE FELT like he was chasing Stardust through their tiny home, trying to stop her progress at every turn. "What do you mean, you're leaving?" he questioned

He felt a sense of panic that he had never felt before. In the short year that they had known each other, Star had become his whole damn world and now, she was packing to leave him.

"I just can't do this anymore," she whispered, tossing her stack of sweaters into the suitcase she was packing.

"Do what? Be in love with me? Live here in this house

with me? What can't you do anymore, Star?" he spat. He had just told her that he loved her for the first time and he was sure that they were on the same page. No, she didn't say the words back but he could tell that she wanted to. He could see how much Star loved him every time they made love. It was right there in her beautiful green eyes, staring back at him.

"I never said that I'm in love with you, Lake," she challenged.

"You don't have to say the words for me to know, Honey. I can see that you love me every time you look at me, Star." She walked back to the bathroom to retrieve the small bag of toiletries she had packed earlier. "Stop running away from me, Star and look at me," he said, grabbing her arm to spin her around to face him. She looked down to where his hand dug into her flesh and back up at him.

"You want to take your hand off of my arm, Lake?" she asked. It sounded more like a warning and less like a question. He sighed and released her, noting that she would probably wear his handprint the next day. Lake instantly regretted his decision to grab her in anger. That wasn't him—it wasn't who he wanted to be. Not anymore. He thought he had worked through all his anger issues when he was a teenager but finding out that his father had a whole different family he never knew about was bringing those feelings of anger and hostility back in full force. He had been seeing a therapist regularly for six months now, trying to work through everything again, but Star walking out on him sent him over the edge.

"I'm sorry," he whispered. "I'd never hurt you, Star. You know that right?" he asked. She looked down at the purple marks on her arm and back up to him as if silently proving him wrong.

"You and I both know what you're dealing with, Lake. I think it would be best if you just let me finish packing my shit and walk out of here. It's for the best. You need to figure out your life and deal with your anger issues. I'm not the woman you want me to be. I can't be the dutiful little woman sitting at home, waiting for you to come back every night. I won't turn into what my parents were, Lake," she whispered. He knew she had a rough childhood and that her parent's marriage was rocky, to say the least, but he and Star weren't her parents. Her mom and dad had been dead for years now but she was still fighting their ghosts for her freedom.

"Is that why you won't tell me that you love me, Star?" he asked. God, he wanted to go to her, pull her against his body, and remind her how good they were together but he also knew Star wouldn't allow it. Not now. Not when her mind was already made up about him.

"I won't give you the words because it's not how I feel about you, Lake," she fibbed.

He looked her over and knew his smile must have looked as mean as it felt, "Liar," he accused. She shrugged as if it wasn't a big deal that he could see right through her.

"Say what you want, Lake. Hell, think whatever you want to about me but let me go, please," she begged. It was the last thing he wanted to do but he had no choice. He was going to lose her either way. Standing clear of her path, to let her walk it alone, was his only option. She wasn't going to change her mind about leaving. He could see it in her eyes as she stared him down. Star had made her decision and when his woman set her mind to something, there would be no changing it. He'd have to let her walk away but he wouldn't stand there and watch her do it. Lake wasn't a martyr.

"Do what you have to do, Star. But, if you leave, do us both a favor and don't come back," he whispered. Lake grabbed his jacket and truck keys and let the screen door slam shut on his way out to his pick-up. He didn't look back, he couldn't because if she was standing in the door watching him leave, he'd turn back and beg her to stay and that wasn't how he wanted her. Lake wanted Star to want to stay with him, not do it out of obligation or pity. No, he'd let her walk, and somehow, he'd find a way to move on.

LAKE SANI SAT in the back of the bar watching her. How could she be there, in the same place as him, after all these years? The last time he saw Stardust Luntz they were both kids. He was just a twenty-four-year-old jerk trying to convince an eighteen-year-old girl to be his. But, fate stepped in and ripped her out of his life, but not from his heart. God, she was still beautiful after all these years. Ten years made him into a miserable asshole who thought he finally had his life figured out, but seeing Star again only proved that he was a damn fool and completely wrong about everything.

Instead of spending the last ten years being with the woman he wanted more than he did his next breath, he let her go. What choice did he have? She forced him to accept the fact that she didn't want anything to do with him by leaving their reservation, their tribe, and the home that they had shared for almost a year. Star left him and he couldn't do a damn thing about it, even if he wanted to.

Lake met her when his life was crazy. He had just found out that his father, Echo, had two other kids—his older sisters, Kaiah and Aylen. They were half shifter, like their dad and half seer, like their mother. His sisters had shown up to help his tribe's former chief when his son was abducted, and they became a permanent fixture in his life. He loved having Kaiah and her husband Gray living just down the street from the small cabin he built. Aylen and her husband Rios came up to Canada every chance they got. Lake loved being an uncle to all his sisters' kids but a part of him longed for everything they both found—someone to share his life with and kids of his own. He thought that Star would be that person for him but he was wrong. All she wanted to do was play house, and when it came right down to it, she didn't like the game. She claimed that he was too controlling, too possessive, and she said that she needed space to find herself. He promised to give her the space she needed; Lake just never imagined she'd need half a country between them to find herself. Last he heard; she was settled down with some hockey player on the East Coast just outside of Vancouver. He missed his chance with Star and there would be no going back to change any of his past, even if he could. Lake might have turned out to be an asshole, but his path was set and all in all, he wouldn't change—not even for another chance with Star.

What he could do was be a gracious host and thank her for coming all the way home to attend his mother's funeral.

His sisters sat at the bar and were whispering with each other and he could tell by their stares that he was the topic of their conversation. Gray found him and clapped his shoulder with his big hand. "You good, son?" he asked. Hearing Gray call him "son" always made him laugh but it also drove home the fact that his father was a no show for his own wife's funeral.

"I will be," Lake lied. "You see my dad?" he asked.

Gray shook his head, "No, sorry," he said. "Kaiah said she knows he's safe but she doesn't see him showing up to this. You know your dad isn't taking Anita's passing well. He just needs some time."

Lake barked out his laugh, "She's his wife—his mate," he said. "Showing up to her funeral isn't a choice. He needs to man up like the rest of us and be here for this."

"You try telling him that?" Gray asked.

"I tried talking to him yesterday but he wasn't up for having a conversation," Lake said.

"Well, you could just demand he show up," Gray said. Yeah, he could demand that his father show up to his mom's funeral, but he shouldn't have to. As his tribe's chief, Echo would have to do as Lake ordered but he never played that card with his father before, and he wouldn't start now. The tribe needed him to be a leader who stood up for the good of the group and did not use his power or position for personal gain. No, he wouldn't order his father to be where he should be and he certainly wouldn't beg.

"I know but me being chief has nothing to do with my father being here for his family. He should want to do that because it's the right thing, not because I've demanded it," Lake said. "I won't abuse my authority like that."

"That's what makes you a damn good chief, Lake," Gray said, slapping his shoulder again.

"Thanks, man," Lake said. "That means a lot coming from you." It did too. Lake had come to love having his sisters and their families in his life. Gray and Rios were pretty cool and he never felt alone anymore—not even on a day like today when he should be feeling just that way.

"Don't look now but you are going to have company in three, two—" Gray waved at him and turned to find his way back to Kaiah's side. Lake thought the old guy was losing his damn mind until he turned around to find Stardust standing behind him.

"Hey," Star whispered to him. He looked her up and down, noting the sexy little black dress she wore, and damn near swallowed his tongue. Ten years had been kind to her—she had curves for miles and was sexier than he ever remembered.

"Hi, Star," he almost whispered. "It's good to see you," he said, clearing his throat.

"You too," she said. "I'm so sorry about your mother, Lake." She reached for his hand and held it for just a minute until he pulled his free.

"Thanks for coming," he said.

"I heard you're chief now," she said, quickly changing the topic.

"Yeah—happened a few years back," he said. They had quite a few changes of power after Jace went to jail for murdering his wife. Hell, Echo even served as chief of their tribe for a couple of years until Lake's mom got sick. When his dad stepped down, Lake agreed to take the position to give his dad time to spend with his mom. They knew that she wouldn't have long and that the more time they had together, the easier letting her go might be. But, he was wrong because his father wouldn't have ever been ready to let his wife go. He had to admit, he didn't mind being chief. Taking on the responsibilities, as his tribe's new leader, might have started as a way to help his dad out but it quickly became so much more to him. He wanted to make a difference in his community and that was what he strived to do every day.

"I always knew how much you loved our tribe, Lake. I'm betting you're a pretty great chief," she said.

"Thanks for saying that," he said. "You sticking around town for a bit or do you have a family to get back to?" he asked. Sure, he was prying but he didn't care.

"No," she said. "I'm newly divorced—well, almost, and it's just me and my son," she whispered.

"Your son?" he asked.

"Yes," she said. "His name is Kai."

"Well, I'm sorry to hear about your divorce," he lied. She smirked up at him, letting him know she wasn't buying his bullshit. "But I hope that you and Kai will stick around town for a while. It would be nice to catch up with you, Star."

STARDUST

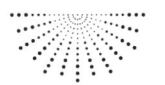

Star made it through the rest of Anita Sani's funeral without chasing Lake around like a lovesick puppy. That was an impressive feat since she wanted to do just that, but she wasn't a kid anymore, and acting like one on her first full day back in town wasn't how she wanted things to go. She wanted to show back up in town with her head held high and her mask perfectly in place. Star didn't want anyone to see what she had been through over the past ten years—that wasn't anyone's business but her own. She was the stupid fool who married the asshole who beat her. She was the idiot who felt she had no other options than to marry him when she turned up pregnant—even after she saw the warning signs. The abuse started before they were even engaged and she ignored the signs, needing for her relationship to work out with Dane. She was pregnant with another man's baby—Lake's baby and letting Dane believe that Kai was his was her biggest mistake. Now, her son had

Dane's last name and thought of him as his father and the last thing she wanted was for her asshole, abusive, soon to be ex-husband hanging around her kid. The only way she'd fix this whole mess was to prove that Lake was Kai's dad, and that would involve some DNA tests. She just hoped like hell that Lake would willingly submit to one because getting a court order would cost money and that was something she didn't have right now. As soon as she asked Dane for the divorce, he froze their joint accounts and left her and Kai penniless. Yeah—he was an ass.

Now, she had to come up with a new plan. Star wasn't looking forward to telling Lake that he had an almost ten-year-old son he didn't know about. Hell, she was going to have to find a way to tell Kai that the man he thought was his father his whole life, was just some hockey player she hooked up with, and then tricked into marrying her. That was on her and something she'd regret for the rest of her life but when she walked away from Lake, ten years back, she thought she had no other path.

Being with Lake had been like living a fairytale, and Star knew from watching her parents that happily ever after's didn't exist for girls like her. She was a shifter who had grown up on a reservation—a far cry from a palace but Lake was her prince and he treated her like his princess. Lake moved into her little house, that her mom had left her when his sisters were helping find Jace's kid. She liked the idea of playing house and having Lake around but when he got serious, a little too fast for her liking, she pushed him away. She came up with some lame excuse of wanting time to figure her shit out, but honestly, she wanted to run as far as she possibly could because Lake was intense. He was talking about marriage, kids, and forever and God that scared the shit out of her. Star closed her little house, packed her suitcase, and took off for parts unknown. She landed in Vancouver and thought about turning back and going home at least a million times a day but then she met Dane.

He was sexy as hell, had charisma for days, and charmed the pants right off her—literally. She liked how he made her no promises because she wasn't ready to give him any. She was still in love with Lake and knew that he'd always hold a piece of her heart. About two months after she moved in with Dane, she found out that she was pregnant and panicked. She told Dane about the baby and when he assumed that the baby was his, she didn't correct him. That was her first mistake and agreeing to marry him was her second.

He had been verbally abusive since day one but then, after she said, "I do," he started slapping her around, getting more physical with her. He'd laugh it off when she'd tell him that his jab to the shoulder hurt, or that she didn't like it when he grabbed her a little too hard. Star should have walked away the first time she landed in the hospital with a broken arm from Dane pushing her up against the wall during a heated argument. But, he showed up to the ER with flowers and seemed to be sorry for what he did. He promised her that he'd never let things get out of hand like that again. He made excuses that it was due to the extreme stress that his team was under to win the cup. He made her pretty promises that he'd change and told her he loved her, and for a while, things were good—until they weren't.

When Dane struck Kai, she couldn't stay with him any longer. She had to get out—not only for her sake but now for her son's. She packed up their things, loaded up the U-Haul truck, and hitched her old car to the back. By the time Star got back to Toronto and opened her little house up, she found out that Lake's mother passed and knew she had to attend Anita's funeral, even if that meant she was going to have to face Lake. She knew that sooner or later; she was going to have to face the shitty mistakes she made in the past, but she was hoping for just a little more time. Now, she was staring at her past and wishing so much that he could be her future, but that was ridiculous. Ten years was a long time to forget someone and Lake had probably forgotten all about her.

He was looking at her with his soulful brown eyes, that always made her a little weak in the knees, and she forgot what he even said. Was he waiting for a response? Had he asked her a question? "I'm sorry, what?" she asked.

Lake's sexy smile was easy and melted her girl parts. "I said that I hope you stick around. It would be great to catch up."

"Oh—yeah," she agreed. "I will be staying—permanently. I moved back into my parent's old house with Kai. It was empty for a few years until I could find renters but when my marriage didn't work out, I gave them notice that I needed to move back. It's nice being back at home," she said. "Kai seems to love the reservation. You still live over there?" she asked, slipping in her nosey question.

Lake chuckled, "Yep," he said. "As chief, I'm expected to live on the reservation."

"Yeah," she breathed. "Sorry, I'm just a little out of it with traveling back from Vancouver, moving everything in, and getting the house set up. It's good to see you again, Lake. I'll see you around, I'm sure," she said, effectively dismissing him.

She felt like a complete idiot for prying into his life but she just couldn't help herself. She had one more question and if she didn't ask it, she'd regret it later. "Are you married?" she asked just as Lake was turning away. He turned back to look at her, a smirk on his handsome face.

"Nope," he said. He crossed his arms over his chest and stared her down as if daring her to ask her next question. She couldn't help herself and she never backed down from a dare.

"You with anyone?" she asked. He threw back his head and barked out his laugh.

"Nope," he said.

Yeah—she might have been a fool but she at least had her answer. "Well, good to know," she said. "I'll see you around, Lake," she promised.

"See you around, Stardust," he agreed, and just those four little words from him gave her so much damn hope, it was ridiculous.

THE NEXT DAY, Star spent most of the morning getting Kai registered for school on the reservation and even took him in to meet his teacher. She couldn't believe that her fourth-grade teacher, Mrs. Washington, was still teaching at the school. A part of Star loved that her son was going to go to the same school that she grew up attending. It was also the same school that Lake went to, although he was five years ahead of her and they didn't hang around each other back then.

After she got Kai settled in his new class, she spent the rest of the morning scouring the help wanted section of the newspaper that the little town still published. Yeah—her community was a throwback, but in a good way after living in a big city, she was ready to slow down to regroup and figure out her next move. It was just what she and Kai needed to move on from the horrible mistakes she made since leaving the reservation ten years prior. Star found a few promising jobs, one being at Kai's school on the reservation as a librarian. She didn't have any job skills in that area since all her jobs involved asking what number meal the customer wanted or which pump they were paying on at the gas station.

When Star left the reservation, she was only nineteen years old and had just barely graduated from high school. She walked away from Lake swearing to herself that she was going to leave town, get her life together, and find a way to put herself through college and get her degree to teach. She wanted to be an elementary school teacher like her grandmother was. It was all she ever wanted to be since she was just a little girl, sitting at her grandmother's kitchen table, "helping" her grade papers. It was more like Star would color a smiley face on the kid's papers while her grandmother did all the heavy lifting and fact-checking. She smiled at the memory of spending time with her grandma—

something she still missed and ached for Kai to have. But, her son would never know his grandmothers. Her mother died just before she turned eighteen and her dad took off. She found out her father had drunk himself to death about a year later and that's when her life started to spiral out of control. That's when Lake told her that he loved her and life started moving too fast. That was when she took off and left the best thing that had ever happened to her—Lake Sani.

Her cell phone rang, pulling her out of her trip down memory lane, and she rummaged through her purse to find it. "Hello," she answered, pressing it to her ear.

"Mrs. Luntz?" a woman asked. Yeah, that wasn't exactly her last name anymore—at least not legally, but there would be no way she'd tell anyone in town that she was married to THE Dane Michaels, the famous hockey player. It was bad enough that she had to tell the school that Kai's last name was Michaels. It should be Sani—like his father's, his real father's. But, she was going to take care of that. She was home to make things right but that meant taking things one day at a time. The least she could do was use her maiden name for herself around town since that's how everyone remembered her. As soon as she could legally change it back, she was going to.

"Yes," Star said. "This is Star."

"Hi, Star. I'm Mrs. Hayward. I'm not sure if you remember me but I was your second-grade teacher."

"Oh my goodness, yes," Star said. "You taught me my times tables," she said.

The woman chuckled into the other end of the phone.

"Yep," she said. "Math is still one of my favorite subjects to teach, although I'm the principal at the school now."

Alarm bells and red flags were waving around her and she panicked. She knew it was too soon to put Kai into school. They had only been in town for a day and a half but she hated having him just sitting around the house being bored while she job hunted and unpacked. Star thought that throwing him into the deep end would help him adapt and swim, but now, she worried that it had just landed him in hot water and that was all her fault.

"What happened?" Star questioned. "What did Kai do?" she asked.

"Oh, yes," Mrs. Hayward said. "I heard that your little boy is now in our little school. It's a full-circle moment for so many young parents when they drop their little ones off here. What grade is Kai in?" she asked.

"Fourth," Star said. "Wait—are you calling about Kai or not?"

"Well, not really. Although, I'm thrilled to have him here in our school. I'm calling for you. I think you filled out an online application this morning, to fill our spot as school librarian."

"Yes, about an hour ago," she said. "Was that all right? I know I don't have much experience—well unless you call working at fast food places and the gas station in town, experience. I'm sorry that I've wasted your time," Star whispered.

"No," Mrs. Hayward said. "Not at all, Stardust. I'd like for you to come in for an interview—at your earliest convenience."

"Really?" Star asked. "You want to talk to me about the librarian job?" She wasn't sure if she wanted to laugh or cry at the absurdity of what she had just said. "You heard the part where I told you that I have no experience, right."

"Yes," Mrs. Hayward said. "I'd love to promise you that it will be as exciting as you're making it out to be, but I'm afraid that it won't be. You'll be in charge of the library and have to conduct story time when the little ones come in, but that's about it. The job will entail just checking books in and out, shelving them—you know basic librarian stuff."

"It sounds wonderful," Star gushed. "When can I come in to interview?"

"Any time you're free. We're looking for someone to start right away," Mrs. Hayward said. "You will be staying in the area, right?"

"Yes," Star said. "I'm home for good." She meant it too because once she figured out how to tell Lake about his son, she wanted to give them time to get to know each other. It was the right thing to do and she hoped it would help give them both back some of the time that she stole from them.

"Well, how about one this afternoon?" Mrs. Hayward asked.

"I'll be there," she breathed. "And, Mrs. Hayward—thank you." Star ended the call and ran back to her bedroom. She needed to find something to wear and get over to the school before her former teacher came to her senses and changed her mind about considering her for the librarian position. This was the first break she had gotten in a damn long time and she didn't want to screw it up.

LAKE

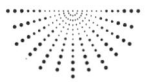

Lake spent most of the day after his mother's funeral in committee meetings. He was board out of his ever-loving mind and completely distracted by thoughts of his former girlfriend. She consumed his dreams last night and every damn waking hour of his day so far. He had missed voting, without being prompted by his secretary twice, and was starting to wonder if everyone else in the room would figure out that his mind was on the woman who still owned a piece of his heart, instead of focusing on his job.

"You okay, boss?" Zoe asked. She wasn't just his secretary; she was one of his best friends from high school and way too qualified to be working for him. But, in their little town, jobs were hard to come by even with a college degree. He knew that Zoe had her BA in Bio-Chemistry and was probably the smartest person he knew. When she moved back to the reservation after graduating from college, Zoe married her high school sweetheart and he owned an electrical business in town that did quite well. Skilled laborers were always needed in their area and her husband, Beau, did well for himself. Zoe agreed to stay on the reservation and took the job as his assistant/secretary as soon as he was appointed chief. He tried to talk her out of it, but she told Lake that she might as well like who she's working for if she was going to have to take a job she was overqualified for. He liked the way she never referred to the position as "beneath her", even if they both knew that it was. It was one of the things he loved about his friend—she wasn't afraid to do the dirty jobs, get down in the trenches with him, and make a change for the better on the reservation. He was hoping to bring his pack and his tribe up to speed with the current century and that was no easy feat. His people were set in their ways and him shaking things up wasn't always welcome around town.

"I'm fine," he lied. "Why?" he questioned. He knew exactly why Zoe was asking, but he wouldn't outwardly admit that he was distracted by a sexy little, dark-haired, wolf shifter, who rode back into town days earlier. Nope—he was just fine.

"Liar," she breathed just loud enough for him to hear. Zoe pretended to cough and it sounded suspiciously like she was saying, "Stardust". Lake shot her a sideways glance and she giggled.

"Listen, everyone," he said, standing from his seat, letting it scrape back over the hardwood floor. "I'd love to take a fifteen-minute break," he said. "I don't know about all of you but I could use a cup of coffee and stretch my legs. Sound good?" he asked. Most of the committee members around the table nodded their agreement and stood to leave the room. He turned back to stare down Zoe who hadn't moved from her seat.

"What the fuck, Zoe?" he asked.

"Why Mr. Sani," Zoe feigned shock, causing him to smile. "Such language in a professional setting. I thought you are the chief, Sir," she teased. Zoe made a tsking sound and shook her head, really driving home her performance. "Not very chief-like, Lake," she accused.

He couldn't help himself; Lake threw back his head and full-on laughed at his friend's theatrics. "You know me better than that, Zoe. I'm anything but 'chief-like,'" he said, using his fingers to form the air quotes he knew she hated. Zoe rolled her eyes and giggled.

"So, you gonna tell me about your little talk with Star, or do you want me to guess how that went? You know everyone around town is whispering about the two of you yesterday at your mom's wake." Lake had heard the rumors about him and Star already circulating the reservation. People loved to talk and when they were given something or in this case, someone to talk about—that was all they seemed to do. There was nothing to talk about though—not that it would stop anyone from spreading false stories about the two of them.

"I've heard the rumors," he grumbled. "Here's the quick run-down." He sat on the corner of the table and stared her down. "She's back in town after a nasty split with her husband, not planning on going back to Vancouver, moving back into her childhood home, is planning on sticking around, and she has a kid. That answer everything for you?" he asked.

"You got all that from a less than five-minute chat?" Zoe countered. He wasn't about to admit that he had stalked her on social media as soon as he got home from his mom's funeral. He'd keep the fact that he spent hours scouring the internet, searching her Facebook, Instagram, and Twitter accounts for any clue as to how she still felt about him, to himself. He looked back years in her search history, trying to find one picture of the two of them together to give him some small glimmer of hope that she at least thought about him in the ten years that she had been gone. But, he found nothing. All he found were smiling, happy faces of her, her supposedly soon to be ex-husband and her adorable kid.

"Yep," he lied again.

"You are the worst liar," Zoe challenged. "It's okay to admit that you have feelings for her, Lake. I remember when she left town. I saw what her leaving did to you and I know it's been ten years but you have to still feel something for her. You're just that kind of guy," she said.

"What kind of guy am I, Zoe?" he asked, sounding a little more pissed-off than he wanted. "Because if you say that I'm a fucking nice guy, I swear—" he didn't finish his threat because it was pointless. She was smiling at him, knowing exactly what he was trying to deny—he was a nice guy and he hated being that person sometimes. Once in a while, he would like to act the selfish bastard and tell people to go fuck themselves, but that wasn't who he was. "Shit," he grumbled under his breath.

"It's okay, Boss," Zoe soothed, her hand on his forearm.

"Fine," he barked. "I have feelings for Star," he just about shouted. "Does that make you happy to hear?" he asked. Zoe's smile quickly faded as she stared past him. Lake stood and spun around to find Stardust standing in the doorway to the conference room they were using for the meeting. "Shit," he shouted. "What the fucking hell did I do to piss off the universe?" he asked.

"Um, I'll just leave you two to talk," Zoe said. She grabbed her things and hurried from the room, like the coward she was, and Lake wanted to tell her not to go. He wanted to demand that she caused this mess and she could stick around to help him clean it up but for some odd reason, he was finding it hard to form words. Oh sure, now he was struck mute when he needed his ability to speak and clear up the mess that had been made.

"I'm sorry to interrupt," Star whispered.

Lake nodded and plastered his best, "What can I do to help you," smile on his face. It was the same one he gave to everyone who stepped into his office. That had to be why she was there—to see him on some official capacity even though he was hoping it was for more. Because God, he wanted more with Star.

"Um, I was told to come here to fill out some paperwork for the school," she squeaked. He hated that she was feeling anxious and shy around him. They should be past all of that —they had a past together, and at least could act as friends now.

"Sure," he said. "How about we go into the other room and I can try to find you the forms you need. What are you looking for exactly?" he asked. Lake put his hand on the small of her back to usher her from the conference room into the main office of the building, and he did his best to ignore the sparks he felt tingling up his arm. It was always like that with Star—like electricity flowing through his veins every time he touched her.

"Well," she said, clearing her throat, "I was just hired as the school's new librarian, and I was sent here to get the background check done—you know for security reasons."

"Wow, Star," he said. "That's great. So, you're settling in well then?" he asked. Sure, he was prying into her business but as a new employee on the reservation, she'd be his "official" business now too.

"Yeah—Kai started school today and has Mrs. Washington," she said. Star giggled and he couldn't help but laugh even though she didn't say anything funny, her laughter was infectious. "I never imagined our kid," Star stopped herself mid-sentence and looked at him. "Um, I mean my kid, going to the same school I did and even having the same teachers." Lake wondered why Star suddenly looked so nervous again. He thought that she had relaxed a little bit around him. "Sorry, can I just get the papers? I need to get back over to the school and pick up Kai so he doesn't have to walk home. He doesn't know his way around the reservation yet."

"Oh, sure," Lake agreed. He handed her the papers that he had been holding. "Just fill these out and bring them back whenever. It usually takes a couple of weeks to come back but if you need a character reference to start, just have Mrs. Hayward call me," he offered.

"Thanks," she said, turning to leave. He wished he had the nerve to ask her out—his head was screaming at him to do it and his heart was begging him to take a leap of faith, but he had gone down that path with Star before and it didn't end well for him.

"Um, the kids in town are working on a special school totem," he said. What the hell was wrong with him? Here he was trying to figure out how to ask her to dinner and his fucking mouth came up with the school project he was in charge of helping with?

"That's nice," she said.

"Yeah—would Kai like to help?" he asked. "Well, I mean, you and Kai could help. We meet Saturday mornings at ten—so tomorrow. It would give you a chance to get to know some of the kids in school, and Kai could make some friends that way. Not that he'll have trouble making friends. I mean I'm sure he's a great kid and all. I mean, his dad's a famous hockey player, right? The kids on the reservation will eat that up," he breathed. Star was staring him down, a knowing smirk on her face and he could tell that he had said too much. Once he started, he couldn't stop. It was almost like he had verbal diarrhea and the words just kept coming and there was nothing he could do to stop them.

"I never told you about Kai's father," she challenged. "How did you know I was married to Dane?" Yeah, this was the part he didn't want to have to admit out loud because it made him sound pathetic.

He winced, "I may have looked you up on Facebook," he admitted, leaving out the part where he stalked all her social media pages. "Sorry," he said.

Star nodded and smiled, "It's all right," she said. "I may have looked you up on Facebook too," she admitted. That little bit of information gave him hope that he knew was ridiculous, but it was there, nonetheless. "Listen," she said, "I can't promise we'll help, but I'll run the idea past Kai and see if it's something he'd like to do. Thanks for the invite," she said. Star turned to leave and smiled back at him over her shoulder. "See you around, Lake," she promised. Lake just stood there like a buffoon, unable to make words again.

THE NEXT DAY Lake woke up early, wanting to head out to the school, and set up before any of the kids showed up. He had slept for shit, up all night again, thinking about Star and their peculiar run in the day before. She had always been an open book but now, she seemed almost reserved and private about her breakup and life out West.

He knew that she probably wasn't going to show up at school this morning, not with the way she ran out of the Town Hall yesterday after he admitted to stalking her online. But, a part of him still hoped she did. It would be nice to meet her son and get to know Star again, especially if they were going to keep running into each other around town.

Gray, Kaiah, and the kids were all at the sight when he got there. He loved that her family was so active on the reservation. And, having a brother-in-law who owned a construction company came in pretty handy, especially as chief. As soon as Lake jumped down out of his truck, he was greeted with his niece's and nephew's shouting his name. He loved being "Uncle Lake". It was one of his favorite roles.

"Hey rugrats," he said, patting them all on their little

heads. He nodded to Ash who had decided to join them. His oldest nephew was in his senior year at the high school and Lake was happy that Ash had shown up. This project was important to the morale of the reservation and something he'd be able to look back on, years from now, with pride.

"Good of you to roll out of bed so early on a Saturday, Ash," Lake teased. He remembered being a teenager and his mother razzing him about sleeping the day away. Just thinking about his mom still made his heartache.

"Chief," Ash nodded and smiled.

Kaiah pulled Lake in for a quick hug. "Don't spook him," she said. "He'll retreat into his dark hole of a room and we'll never see him again. Unless he smells food or a girl calls—then he usually springs back to life." Ash rolled his eyes and grumbled something about Kaiah being lame and Lake laughed.

"How about you take lead on painting today? You know where the paint is right?" Lake asked Ash. His nephew smiled and nodded, going off to find the supplies they used for painting the totem.

"So, how are you holding up?" Kaiah mock whispered. He watched as Gray rounded up his pups by promising them time on the playground. He was carrying the youngest addition and she was fussing at him.

"Don't worry about me," Lake told his sister. "I think the real person you should be worried about is your husband dealing with all those kids," he said, laughing at his brother-in-law's unsuccessful attempts at corralling the unruly kids. Kaiah giggled and shook her head.

"Yeah—they're a handful," she said.

"You're about up to enough kids to have your own hockey team now, aren't you?" Kaiah shot him a look that let him know she wasn't amused by her brother's comment.

"Well, you pop them out two at a time and that's what happens," she grumbled. Besides her and Gray adopting Ash when he was about seven, they had three sets of twins, and their youngest daughter—Rayne. Kaiah was such a good mom, but he knew that she had to be overwhelmed dealing with them all. "You're avoiding my question," she said.

"Sorry—you asked a question?" he asked.

"You know damn well that I did," she said. One of Kaiah's three-year-old boys ran circles around Gray shouting, "Damn," and he shot his wife a look.

"Sorry," she shouted to him, shrugging at her husband. Gray smiled and shook his head at her.

"Our swear jar is going to be nice and full for our family vacation this year," Gray teased.

"Yeah, yeah," Kaiah grumbled, turning her attention back to her brother. "So, how are you doing, Lake? Your mom just passed and no one would blame you for taking a few days to grieve," she said.

"You were in my head again, weren't you?" he asked.

"Maybe," she said. "But, I'm also your older, wiser, and very beautiful sister, and I know you," she said.

"Well, older—sure," he teased. "You're not ugly, but I'm pretty sure wiser is a bald-faced lie," he said. Kaiah smirked and slapped his arm.

"Shut up," she whispered.

"We don't say shut up," Gray shouted back over his shoulder. "It's not nice to say," he reminded his wife.

"Fine," she spat. "Please be quiet," she said to Lake. When he was about ready to laugh at Gray giving her shit, she leaned into Lake's body and pointed her finger into his chest. "Don't test me, fucker," she whispered under her breath to be sure her husband and children couldn't hear her. Lake held up his hands as if in defense and smiled at his sister.

"Got it, Sis," he said.

"Just tell me how you're holding up so we can move on with other more pleasant conversation," she ordered.

"I'm all right," he said. "I mean, I miss her but you could probably pick up on that. Mom was sick for a long time and I'm just glad she's finally at rest," Lake admitted. He truly felt that his mother was in a better place now. She had suffered so much and watching her fight the pain just to stick around for him and his father, was almost unbearable.

"You hear from Dad?" Kaiah asked as if she was reading his mind again.

"No," Lake breathed. "Not for days now. It's like he's dropped off the planet."

"His wife just died a few days ago. How about we cut him a break?" Kaiah asked.

"I don't think that asking a man to show up for his wife's funeral is a stretch," he grumbled.

"True," Kaiah agreed. "Dad and your mom had a special connection and I know he loved her with all he had. He's trying to deal with losing his mate the best he can, Lake. If anything ever happened to Gray, I'd hide away and not want to resurface knowing he wasn't in the world anymore. I'm sure that someday, you'll know how much losing a mate will feel, although I wouldn't wish it on my worst enemy. Just try to remember that and cut dad some slack," she said. Lake wanted to protest and tell his sister that he had already lost his mate because when Stardust left him, she ripped his heart out. But, this wasn't the same because his mother wasn't coming back—she was gone forever. Knowing that Star was alive in the world, no matter how many hundreds of miles away, gave him some comfort. It still hurt like hell knowing that she didn't want him anymore and that their relationship was disposable to her.

As if he had conjured her up by just thinking about her, Star drove down the gravel road to the back parking lot at the school. Seeing her around the reservation again, after all these years, made him feel like a teenage boy—butterflies in the pit of his stomach and all.

"I'll try to ease up on Dad," Lake agreed. He didn't want to talk about his mother's death or his father's complete denial and lack of empathy in front of Star and he hoped Kaiah would catch on.

"Hey," Star said, "am I in the right place?" she asked.

"Yep," Lake said. Her son jumped down from her mom's ancient pick-up and nervously looked around. Lake felt for the kid—it must suck to be the new guy in town, trying to make friends.

"You must be Kai," Lake said, holding out his hand for the kid. "I'm Lake Sani, an old friend of your moms." Kai seemed hesitant about taking Lake's offered hand, finally nodding and reaching for it.

"I'm Kai Michaels," he mumbled as he shook Lake's hand.

"It's good to meet you, Kai," Lake said.

"He's the chief here on the reservation," Star boasted, and Lake rolled his eyes.

"I don't go around telling people that, Star," he teased. "But, I am."

"You didn't tell me you know the chief," Kai said to his mom as if she had wronged him in some way for not telling him that.

"Yep," she said. "Mr. Sani and I grew up together."

Lake winced at the way she used his last name and called him "Mister", around her son. "You can call me Lake if you'd like," he offered. Kai's smile broadened and he nodded.

"I'm Lake's sister, Kaiah," she said holding out her hand to the kid. He smiled and shook her hand and Kaiah gasped. Lake knew that meant she had probably seen something but his sister was good at hiding it from others. "It's nice to meet you, Kai," she said. Kaiah looked past him to where Star stood by her truck and nodded. "Nice to see you again, Star. I hear you're the school's new librarian. Congratulations on your job."

"Yeah—I forgot how quickly news travels around this town. Thanks, I'm excited about it. I'm looking forward to settling in here and building a life for me and Kai," Star said.

"Why don't you go on over and join some of the other kids by the school? You can help Kaiah's son, Ash, with painting if you'd like," Lake said to Kai. He waved at his mother and took off in the direction of the other kids who were starting to show up and gather around the totem that they were working on.

"I guess I better get over there and 'supervise'," Lake said, using his fingers to make air quotes around the word, supervise. Star giggled. "You coming?" he asked her.

"I'd love a few minutes with Star to catch up," Kaiah said. Lake stared down Kaiah as if silently warning her not to ask Star a million questions or stick her nose in Star's business. But, he also knew that his sister planned on doing just that. She had seen something when she touched Kai and Lake wondered what it was.

"Oh, well, sure," Star stammered. "I'd like that." Lake started for the schoolhouse and turned back to shoot Kaiah one last warning glance, even mouthing, "Be nice," to her behind Star's back. She rolled her eyes at him and waved him on as if telling him to get lost. He wasn't sure that leaving Star to fend for herself with Kaiah was a good idea or not but his sister wasn't giving him a choice. One thing was clear —Star said she was sticking around and building a life for her and Kai in town and that news had him hoping for possibilities he didn't allow himself to dream of.

STARDUST

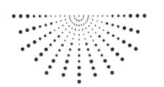

"You guys getting settled all right?" Kaiah asked. Star wasn't sure why Kaiah had suddenly taken an interest in her or her moving back home. She never seemed to have any interest in getting to know Star when she and Lake were together. If she remembered correctly, Kaiah and her sister Aylen didn't seem to approve of her and Lake being together, but maybe time had changed Kaiah's assessment of her.

"Yes," Star said. "Everyone's been so nice and welcoming. I got my mother's things out of storage, including her old pick-up over there," Star said, pointing back to her truck. She used to love that truck and when she moved, she put it into storage with the rest of her mom's stuff, getting the cabin ready to rent. It was nice to have her mother's old things around—made the cabin feel more like home.

"That's great," Kaiah said, although her tone told Star that she wasn't as enthusiastic as she was pretending to be.

"What's up, Kaiah?" Star asked, getting right to the point. She was never one to beat around the bush and if Kaiah had something to say, she might as well not waste either of their time and just come out with it.

"I guess I could ask you that same question, Star," Kaiah countered.

"I'm not following, but if you have something to say to me, please just say it. I came here today to help my son get acquainted with the town and hopefully make a few new friends, not to stand here and play twenty questions with someone who doesn't like me," Star accused.

"I like you just fine, Star," Kaiah challenged. "You bring Kai here to spend time with his dad, too?" she asked. Star squinted her eyes at Lake's sister. She knew who Kaiah was and what she could do, but Star wouldn't admit to anything unless Kaiah came out and point-blank asked her.

"His father is back in Vancouver," Star said, playing dumb.

"You and I both know that's a lie," Kaiah whispered. She leaned in closer to Star and looked around before saying the rest. "You never told Lake he's a father?" she accused. Shit—she knew, and from the anger that flashed across Kaiah's face, she knew all of it.

"You got all of that from just shaking my kid's hand?" Star asked.

"Yes," Kaiah said. "Ten years is a long time, Star. My abilities have only gotten stronger. How could you do that to him?" Kaiah asked. "He had a right to know that he was going to be a father. All this time—wasted because you met some other guy? Does your ex know he's not Kai's father?"

Kaiah asked. Star looked around to make sure no one was listening and back to her.

"Please lower your voice," Star begged. "Yes, he knows. It's part of the reason we left. Kai doesn't know and well, things with Lake were complicated when I found out I was pregnant. I couldn't just call him up out of the blue and tell him he was going to be a father. I plan on telling him and Kai the truth. It's one of the reasons I came back home. I just need time," she whispered.

"How much time are we talking?" Kaiah asked. "You've already had ten years."

She deserved that remark and more. Kaiah was right—she should have found a way to tell Lake about his son. Each year that passed, she vowed to herself that she was going to tell him. She would work up her courage and even dialed his cell number into her phone a few times only to delete it and chicken out. As the years went by, she felt less and less sure of herself. Telling Lake became more of an if, rather than a when, and eventually, she decided that so much time had passed, it would be pointless to fill him in. Sure, he had a right to know but she had already robbed him of so much time with Kai, she worried that Lake wouldn't be able to find a way to forgive her for keeping his son from him.

"A couple of weeks?" Star questioned.

"No," Kaiah said. "You need to tell him this week. I'll give you five days, Star. My brother is still in love with you, even if he hasn't admitted it to himself yet. He's going to ask you out to dinner and when he does, I want you to say, yes. You can use that opportunity as your 'perfect time' to tell him. That's what you've been waiting for, right? The perfect time to tell Lake that he has a nine-year-old kid?" Star nodded and looked over to where Kai was helping Ash paint and sighed.

"I'll have to tell Kai too," Star murmured.

"It's only fair to them both," Kaiah said. "Give Lake a chance to know his son and Kai some time to know his father—his real father. It's only right, Star." Kaiah turned to walk over to her husband and kids, "Oh, and if you chicken out again," she said, letting Star know that she had read her earlier thoughts, "I'll tell him myself." Star watched as Kaiah walked away and she felt a wave of panic that made her want to vomit. She needed to get out of there and take a few minutes to calm down. It was the only way she'd figure out how to approach her next move.

She walked across the parking lot to her truck and almost made it into the cab before Lake stopped her. "Hey," he breathed, jogging over to her. "You're not sticking around?"

"I, um—I'm not feeling so great right now. I skipped breakfast and I'm regretting that decision. You mind if I head home to grab a bite to eat? I can be back in time to pick up Kai when this is all over." Lake looked her up and down and she hated the concern she saw on his handsome face. She didn't deserve it—not after everything she had done to him, everything she had kept from him.

"You sure you're all right?" he whispered, looking back at his sister. "Did Kaiah say or do anything to upset you?" he asked.

"No," she quickly breathed. "No, it's not that. I'm just feeling a little sick to my stomach. Nothing that some toast and tea won't fix."

"I can bring Kai home if you'd like. My house is just down the road from yours—it's on the way," he promised. Star sighed and nodded. She was going to have to get used to Kai and Lake spending time together after she spilled the beans in five days.

"I'd appreciate that," she agreed. "Thank you." She climbed into her mom's old truck and slammed the door shut. Star pulled out of the parking lot not bothering to look in her rearview to see if Lake was watching her leave—he was. She could feel his eyes on her—his and Kaiah's and all she could think about was the fact that in just five short days, her life was going to change forever. In just five days, she was going to have to hurt the man she still loved and wanted, and the little boy who owned her whole heart.

STAR HAD CALMED down some since returning home earlier, and she even had a few minutes to shift and go for a quick run. It was something she had missed out in Vancouver. Dane knew she was a shifter but she never felt comfortable with that part of her life around him. He made her feel ashamed of who and what she was, but she chose to live with that shame and guilt rather than leave him. God, she was a fool. It wasn't until Kai started shifting that Dane began coming around and asking questions about her world. He never asked the big questions though and that was how she had kept her secret for so long.

Star was unpacking the rest of her kitchen boxes when she heard Lake's truck pull into her driveway. She tossed the contents onto the counter and went to meet her son at the front door. Star found the two of them walking up to the porch laughing about something and God, the sight of them both together did strange things to her heart. Kai looked so much like Lake she was amazed that neither of them had guessed the truth yet.

"Well, there's my favorite guy," she said, pulling Kai in for a hug. Star didn't miss the flash of disappointment on Lake's face. "You have fun?" she asked.

Kai nodded, "I made a friend and everything," he gushed. Star giggled. It was the first time in weeks that her son sounded excited about anything.

"That's great," she said. "How about you go and get washed up? I'm about to order us some pizza for dinner and you can pick the toppings."

Kai fist-bumped the air and cheered. Her kid did love his pizza. "Can Lake stay for dinner?" he asked.

"Oh," Star said. "I'm sure Lake has better options than pizza takeout for dinner." Kai groaned his disappointment and Lake laughed.

"Pizza sounds pretty good," he said. "If it's all right with you, Star. I'll even treat. Consider it my welcome home gift." Lake stared her down as if challenging her to shoot him down and she nodded. Lake knew her well enough to know that she wouldn't back down from a challenge or a dare.

"Well, that's nice of you," she said. "But, don't feel obligated if you have plans," she said. Star wondered if this was the "dinner date" that Kaiah was referring to during their earlier chat. She told Star to accept his dinner invitation and tell him during their meal, but she couldn't have meant tonight, right? Star was nowhere near ready to spill her guts and tell Lake the truth about Kai. A part of her was hoping that he and her son would get to know each other a little, and that would help soften the blow of finding out that he had a son she never told him about. Kai was an awesome kid, and if Lake got to know him, he'd fall in love with his son—she just knew it.

"Nope," Lake said. "I'm free all night and since tomorrow's not a school day or a workday, why don't we rent a movie and make it a real date?" he asked. She cringed at the mention of their pizza night turning into a date. Kai cheered again and she knew that there would be no saying no to either of them.

"Sounds good," she lied. "Come on in." She held the door open for Lake and he followed her into her cabin. He knew his way around since he used to live there with her, but she still felt like he was a stranger in her home. Honestly, Lake was a stranger to her now, and Star hated that their relationship had come to that. But, that was on her. She was the one who walked away and now, she was going to be the one to destroy whatever was left of their relationship. Just not tonight—she couldn't tell him the truth tonight. It was too soon and tonight she wanted to relax and just enjoy being home. Star could just worry about upending her world later—in five days, to be exact.

LAKE

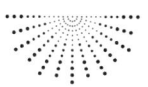

They decided to watch a classic and after a heated debate with Star, they settled on The Goonies. Star tried claiming that The Breakfast Club was a better eighties movie, but he had a swing vote—Kai. Star's son chose pirates and kids going on an epic adventure over his mother's suggestion, but she didn't seem too upset. He was a pretty cool kid and reminded Lake so much of Star. By the time they finished the movie, most of the pizza was gone, and Kai had fallen asleep on his mother's shoulder. Star wrapped an arm around her son and snuggled him into her side.

"He's almost as big as you are," Lake whispered.

Star sighed and kissed the top of his head, "I know," she said. "And, moment's like these are few and far between. He's always so busy, running around trying to keep up with the other kids, and when I do get my hands on him, he complains that I'm smothering him."

Lake chuckled, remembering his mother saying the same thing. "My mother used to say something similar, about me," he said. "I used to wipe off her kisses and tell her not to hug or kiss me in front of my friends," he whispered. He'd give just about anything now to kiss and hug his mother just one more time.

"How are you doing with everything?" Star asked.

"Coping," he admitted. "Barely. I watched her suffer for so long, that I wished that it would end. I feel like the world's most awful son for thinking things like that but I know she wouldn't want me to feel that way. I just hope she's in a better place with no more pain or suffering," he said. "I miss her though."

"Missing her won't ever go away," Star said. "It just becomes more manageable. When my mom died I was so lost. I didn't know what to do with my life, but I knew that whatever I did, she'd want me to be happy. I just got through one day at a time and after a while, I realized I felt less grief when I thought about her. I didn't focus on the sad memories, but the happier ones, you know?" she asked.

"I'm looking forward to that happening to me. I'm still focused on the sadness, but work helps, and spending days like today helps too. I enjoyed spending the evening with you and Kai," he said. "Thank you for inviting me to pizza night."

"Well, thanks for treating and turning it into eighties movie night too," Star said. "I'm sure I'll be hearing never-ending stories about deadly pirates and pirate ships for the next few weeks."

Lake smiled and looked the boy over, "He's a great kid,

Star. You've done a good job with him. I'm sure these last few weeks haven't been easy for either of you," he whispered.

"No," she said. "They have not, but we'll find our way through. Moving back here was a good first step."

"First step?" he asked.

"Yeah," she said. "My plan has a few steps to it." She squinched up her nose and smiled at him and Lake thought it was the cutest thing he'd seen in a damn long time. But, he couldn't start thinking about Star like that—not anymore. Time had changed them both. She was a mother now, and he was chief of his pack and tribe, with responsibilities that didn't include chasing around the prettiest girl in town. That was his old life but when Star left town, she took that life with her.

"Well, I hope it all works out for you both, Star," Lake whispered. She was so close to him on the sofa that all he had to do was reach out and touch her but Lake knew if he did, he wouldn't want to stop.

"Thank you, Lake," she said. "I appreciate that and everything from today. It was good for Kai to get out there and make some friends." Star pulled free from her son and stood. "I better get him back to his bed." She bent to pick him up and Lake reached out to her, placing a hand on her arm, stopping her.

"I can carry him back to his bed," he offered. "Like I said earlier, he's almost as big as you are." Star giggled and nodded.

"Thanks," she said. "I'm pretty sure he's the reason my back constantly hurts these days. He's always falling asleep on the sofa and I have to lug him back to his room."

"No problem," Lake said. He stood and pulled Kai into his arms, cradling his limp body against his chest.

"He's in my old bedroom," she said. "You remember the way?" Star asked. He remembered the way back to her room. When they lived in the cabin together, it was the room that they shared. Star always said she felt weird sleeping in her parent's old room so, she opted to use her childhood bedroom.

"Yep," he said. "Be right back." He carried Kai back down the small hallway and found his room. A few moving boxes were lining the wall, but Star had done a nice job getting Kai's room together. He put the boy in his bed and watched as he stirred and then snuggled under his blankets. Watching Star's son, Lake wondered if she hadn't left town ten years ago if he might not be tucking his own child into his bed now, but that was just a crazy pipe dream because she did leave. She found that dream with another man and Lake needed to remember that. Still, he was foolish enough to hope again and that was dangerous. Hope with Star led to heartbreak and that wouldn't be something he could go through again.

He walked back through the small cabin to find Star in the kitchen washing the dinner dishes. "No dishwasher?" he asked.

"Nope," she grumbled. "You know my mother always said that someday when she made it big, she'd get us a dishwasher and well, that never happened. I don't mind it since it's just me and Kai." Lake picked up the dishtowel from the counter and took a plate from her. "You don't have to do that," she protested.

"I don't mind. It's the least I can do since I crashed your dinner plans," he said.

"Well, you did pay for the pizza—so I'd call us even," she said.

Lake dried the plate and took the next one from her. All this domesticity had him thinking about things that were better left alone but he couldn't help himself. "I had a nice time tonight," he said.

"Me too," she agreed. "It was nice catching up with you, Lake."

"Go out with me," he said. It sounded more like an order than it had, as the words played through his mind, before leaving his lips. Star handed him the last plate and dried her hands on the towel she was using, making no move to give him an answer.

"I'm not sure that's such a good idea, Lake," she whispered. "We're not the same people anymore and I—" he didn't let her finish her thought. Lake put the plate down on the counter and tossed the dishtowel on top. He pulled her up against his body and sealed his mouth over hers when she looked ready to protest. Lake took his time kissing her, remembering all the little breathy moans and sighs that used to turn him completely on—and they still did. He wanted her, that much was still clear, but she was right. They needed to take things slow, and remember that for whatever reason, they didn't work out the first time they tried all of this. He broke their kiss leaving them both breathless and smiled down at her.

"Just tell me yes," he demanded. "It's just dinner, not a lifetime commitment," he teased. Lake was pretty sure he knew how she felt about commitments. At least, he thought he did. Ten years ago, telling her that he was in love with her, was the first step in the deterioration of their relationship. That's why it hurt so much when he heard, months later, that she was engaged to some hockey player out on the West Coast. He could accept that Star didn't want a commitment but knowing that she agreed to one with a man she only knew for a few months, felt like a knife to the gut.

"Fine," she whispered. "I'll go to dinner with you, Lake." He smiled and she held up her hand as if halting his joy. "I'm only going out with you because we have some things to talk about."

"Like?" he asked.

"How about we just save it for our dinner conversation?" she said. Star was carefully avoiding the use of the word "date," and he wondered what he'd have to do to convince her that's what their dinner was.

"Fine," Lake said. "How about tomorrow night?" he asked.

"Sunday?" she asked. "Well, it's a school night and I don't have anyone to watch Kai," she protested.

"Ash 'kid sits', as he likes to call it. He's good with the little kids and he and Kai hit it off today. How about I get him to come over and hang out with Kai?" he asked. Star looked hesitant and when she nodded her agreement, he blew out his breath not realizing that he had been holding it.

"Really?" he questioned.

"Sure," she agreed. "It will be nice to go out and we need to talk Lake." That was the second time she brought that up, and he was starting to wonder if he was going to like their topic of conversation.

"I can pick you up around five," he offered. "That way I can drop Ash off here and you won't have to worry about a thing."

"Thanks," she said. "I'll be ready at five."

STARDUST

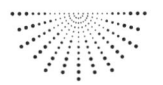

She tried on four different outfits, which was no small feat since she only owned a handful of clothes right now. When she took off from her home with Dane, she worried that he would come home early and realize she was leaving him and taking her son. The last thing she needed was another showdown with Dane in front of Kai. Her son had been through so much already. So, she packed as much as she could, concentrating on Kai's needs for their trip, and decided that if Dane wouldn't send her things, she'd make-due with what she had.

It was worth it—she and Kai got out of Vancouver and by the time she pulled onto the reservation, her lawyer had served Dane with divorce papers that she had drawn up before leaving town. He called her telling her to get her ass home—even threatening to find her and drag her home by the hair if she refused. He told her that she was no one and had no right to walk away from him, taking his son. That was when she informed her asshole ex that he wasn't her son's father. Yeah—it was a jerk move but one that he had coming.

Just after she gave birth to Kai, Dane had come to the hospital, half-drunk and smelling like another woman. She pretended not to notice because leaving him wasn't an option. Dane had guessed that the baby wasn't his. It was almost comical watching him try to do the math to figure out if they were together nine months prior. She could answer that question easily—they weren't. She was with Lake nine months prior but none of that mattered anymore. She chose to leave that life for her new one and there would be no going back to her old life.

Back then she thought of Dane as her savior. He put a roof over her head and took care of her and Kai financially. He was an up and coming hockey player and women practically threw themselves at the players. It didn't matter if they were married or had families waiting for them at home. Not all the players cheated but when the hockey bunnies threw themselves at her husband, Dane didn't miss. He promised her that he'd never do that to her but she knew. Star just chose to look the other way, just like when he started smacking her around. It usually happened when his team was on a losing streak or his coach complained that Dane wasn't performing as he should. He took out his aggression on her, and she became his punching bag, and something she regretted letting happen. Leaving her life in Vancouver, and her relationship with Dane behind was the best decision she had made for her and her son. Star had made so many mistakes over the past ten years but now, she was going to have the chance to make them all right. Tonight, she was going to tell Lake the truth about Kai, and then, she'd deal with telling her son. It was the right thing to do and she wasn't going to falter.

Lake knocked on her door and Kai ran to answer it. She smiled at the way he fist-bumped Kai, causing him to giggle. Her son didn't do enough of that lately and she was happy that he and Lake were getting off on the right foot together. It would be important in their relationship moving forward. She hoped the two of them would be close but she wasn't going to force either of them to do something they didn't want.

"Hey," Lake breathed looking her up and down. She used to love it when he looked at her that way like he wanted her more than his next breath. Lake always made her feel special —loved even, and she was such a fool to walk away from him.

"Hey, back at you," she teased. "You clean up nice, Lake," she said.

"Thanks—you look fantastic," he said. Star ran her hands down her body, noting the way his gaze followed them, and looked back up at him and smiled.

"Really?" she squeaked. "I don't have many wardrobe options," she said. Ash pushed past Lake and stood in her doorway. "Hey, Ash," she said. "Thanks so much for watching Kai tonight."

The kid nodded and smiled, "Lake promised pizza for dinner and I never miss pizza night," Ash said. "Plus, Kai's a pretty cool kid," Ash said, nodding at her son. Kai's smile lit up her tiny cabin and she couldn't help but do the same.

"Let me show you around and make sure you have all the phone numbers you'll need before we head out," she offered. Ash followed her into the kitchen and she went over everything with him. While she did, Lake ordered them some pizza and paid for it by phone, while Kai listened on and gave orders of what toppings to put on the pizza. She giggled to herself at how bossy her son was with Lake. It meant that he felt comfortable with him and that was nice to see.

"Ready?" Lake asked, holding out his hand to her.

"Yep," she agreed. Star reached for Lake's hand and smiled back at Ash and Kai who were already playing video games.

"You two behave," Lake shouted back over his shoulder. "Lock up behind us and only answer the door for the pizza delivery guy," he quickly added. Ash nodded and waved over his shoulder as they left. "You think he got any of that?" he asked.

"Nope," she giggled. "Boys are notorious for their selective hearing," she teased.

"I'm sorry, what?" he questioned, cupping his hand to his ear. She slapped at his arm and giggled.

"So, where are you taking me?" she asked. Lake opened his truck door and helped her up into his pick-up.

"One of my favorite places," he said. "You up for an adventure?" Star eyed him suspiciously, not sure if she trusted him to take her on one of his adventures. She knew that Lake used to be into some pretty crazy stuff—skydiving, rock climbing, bungee jumping. All things she had no interest in doing ten years ago. Now, as a mom, she didn't want to take any chances with all the crazy crap he liked.

"I don't know," she said, squinching up her nose at him.

"Oh come on, Star," he said, "live a little."

"Fine," she agreed. "But remember, I have to start my new job tomorrow and it's a school night, so I can't be out too late," she reminded.

"Right," he said. "I've never dated a mom before," he said, screwing up his face trying to make her laugh. Hearing him call tonight a date made her tummy feel like it was full of butterflies.

"That's what this is?" she asked. "A date?"

"Well, I did ask you to go on a date with me and well, yeah. I consider this a date. How about you let me know what you think after you see where I'm about to take you. You might not think it's a date by the time tonight's over," he said.

"Now I'm worried," she sassed. "Should I be worried?"

Lake chuckled and reached across his seat for her hand, taking it into his own. "Naw," he said. "I shouldn't make you nervous at all, Star. It's just me," he whispered. He was right—it was just him and her—the two of them. Star knew Lake better than she knew most people. They shared a year of their lives together, and even though he didn't know it—they shared a son. They rode in silence the rest of the way up the mountain. He was taking her to the very edge of the reservation's land. She knew the spot once he started heading east and the idea of Lake taking her back to the place that locals called, "The Bluffs," made her smile. They used to go out there and park to make out when they wanted privacy. They would shift and run out, spending most of the night naked under the stars. It was always perfect out there with

Lake, and those nights remained some of her favorite memories with him.

"You're taking me to The Bluffs, aren't you?" she asked.

"I thought it would be appropriate since we had our first date there," he said. "That okay by you?"

She nodded and smiled, "Sounds perfect. I haven't been out here for so long. Do local kids still come out here to make out?" she asked.

Lake squeezed her hand into his and laughed, "Local adults come out here to make out still. At least, I'm hoping that's how tonight is going to end." Hearing Lake admit that he was thinking about making out with her did wicked things to her girl parts.

"That depends on if you still plan on feeding me," she teased. Lake pulled onto the side of the makeshift road. Most of the roads and paths up this way were gravel or dirt, and there weren't any clear-cut parking spots. He unbuckled his seatbelt and reached into the back seat, pulling a picnic basket into the front of the cab.

"I made us a picnic dinner," he said.

"You made dinner?" she questioned remembering what a lousy cook Lake was. "You take cooking classes while I was away?" she teased.

Lake rolled his eyes and smiled at her, "Just look in the basket," he said. She took the picnic dinner from him and sat it on her lap to peek inside.

"You went to Gino's and got us subs?" she just about moaned when the aroma of the fresh, hot subs hit her nose. "They were my favorite. You know, I tried to find subs out in Vancouver that was as good, and I couldn't. Hell, I didn't even find subs that were half this good." She pulled out one of the subs, wrapped in the white paper, that she remembered they used. Lake had them write her name on the side of it, just like he used to and she smiled. Star held it up to her nose and sniffed it, causing him to laugh.

"You want me to give the two of you a few minutes together?" he asked. "I mean, I can come back later if you need some privacy."

Star giggled and put her sub back into the basket. "Tell me we don't have to go on a long hike before I get to eat this thing," she said.

"Only a few miles," he said. Star must have looked at him as if he lost his ever-loving mind. Lake chuckled and got out of his truck, rounding the front to get her door for her. "Just kidding," he said. He pulled the tarp off the back of the truck to reveal that he had put a mattress in the back and even threw blankets and pillows back there. It looked so cozy.

"A night under the stars?" she asked.

"Well, a partial night," he said. "My date has a kid and it's a school night." Lake helped her up into the back of his pickup and followed her up. "I was hoping you'd like my idea," he whispered, pulling the blanket up her legs. "Sorry, I didn't think about it being so cold," he admitted.

"I don't mind the cold," she said. "And, I think that your idea is fantastic."

"Thanks," he whispered. Star took the picnic basket from him and opened it again.

"Please tell me we can eat now," she begged. Lake chuckled and nodded. Star didn't hide how happy his agreement made her, squealing and clapping. She reached into the basket and handed him the sub with his name written on the white paper that it was rolled in. They ate in silence, and Star liked that the silence wasn't something that either of them felt the need to fill. She had been on awkward dates before she met Lake when she was still a young girl. Star always felt so awkward when neither she nor her date had anything to say. She was a nervous rambler, always trying to fill the silence with idle chit chat. With Lake, she didn't feel the need to do that. She was comfortable with him and that had to count for something. At least, it did to her.

"This is nice," she said. "Thank you for inviting me to dinner."

"Well, thanks for agreeing to have dinner with me," he said. He took her trash from her and tossed it back into the basket. "You have time for some good old fashioned star gazing like we used to do up here?" Lake asked. Star nodded and snuggled into his side and shivered. "Here," he said, pulling the covers up over her body.

She wrapped herself around him, soaking up his warmth. "I usually never get cold," she said. "But, Vancouver is a bit warmer than it is out here."

"I bet moving back here has been quite a culture shock for both you and Kai. At least you knew what you were getting used to coming home," he said. Yeah, Star knew exactly what she was getting into by coming back home. Lake stroked his big hand up her back and slid it under her sweater. "I missed you, Star," he whispered into her hair, kissing her forehead.

"I missed you too, Lake," she said. It was the truth. Every time she looked at her son, seeing Lake's eyes looking back at her, her heart ached. "I think we should talk," she said. It was time for her to come clean and give Lake the truth.

He rolled her under his big body and smiled down at her. "How about we get to the make-out portion of the night, and then we can talk on the way home? I don't want to waste any time with you, Star," he whispered. Lake sealed his mouth over hers and kissed her like it had been a hundred years since he last had his lips on her and not just ten. "God, I've missed you," he whispered against her lips.

"Same," she murmured against his mouth. "So much," she said. Star ran her hands through his hair, pulling him down for another kiss.

"You should tell me to stop now," Lake said. He sounded like he was begging her to say those words to him, but she wasn't about to. She wanted him just as much as he seemed to want her.

"I won't," she said, shaking her head. "I want you, Lake." He groaned into her mouth, his hands working down her body to slip her sweater up over her head. Lake quickly stripped her as her greedy hands roamed his bare upper body. He worked his jeans down his body, and she couldn't take her eyes off him. Star had forgotten how beautiful his body was and now, she couldn't seem to get enough of him.

"Shit," he grumbled. "The condoms are in the glove box." He looked at the tiny window in the back of his truck's cab and she giggled.

"I don't think you'll fit," she said, wrapping her arms around his neck. "Besides, I'm on the pill." Lake's face lit up like a kid on Christmas and she giggled again.

"You sure?" he asked. He had only taken her one other time without a condom—the night they made Kai.

"I'm sure," she whispered. "Take me Lake," she begged. "Make me yours again." Lake didn't seem to hesitate or need to be asked twice. He nudged the head of his cock through her wet folds.

"Fuck," he breathed. "You're so wet for me already." She moaned and shamelessly rubbed her wet folds over his dick.

"Please," she begged. Lake thrust into her body and still when she cried out. He didn't give her much time to adjust to his size before he started moving inside of her again.

"You feel so fucking good," he moaned. Lake palmed her taut nipples, sucking them both into his warm mouth, one at a time. The cold air hitting them after was a nice shock to her overly sensitive skin, and Star knew she was close to finding her release.

"I'm going to come, Lake," she shouted. His wolfish grin in place, she could tell that he was determined to drag it out and make her beg him for her release. It was a little game that they used to play and she knew that he wanted to play. "Lake," she warned.

"Tell me you'll go out with me again, Baby. Agree to another date with me," he insisted. Lake stilled inside of her and she knew he wasn't going to give her what she wanted without her agreement.

"Lake, please move," she begged. "I need to come."

"I know, Baby," he soothed. Lake pushed her long, dark hair back from her face and cupped her jaw. "Promise me that you'll go out with me again," he ordered. Lake kissed his way down her neck to her breasts again, gently grazing his teeth over her sensitive nipples.

"Lake," she cried out.

"I believe the words you are looking for are, 'Yes, I'd love to go out with you again.'," he teased. Star wiggled under his big body and he stilled again.

"I'd love to go out with you again, Lake," she breathed.

"See, was that so hard?" he quipped.

"Lake," she growled in warning, her inner wolf showing her claws. He chuckled and pulled almost completely out of her body only to thrust balls deep back into her.

"I'll give you what you want, Honey," he promised.

"About time," she grumbled. He laughed again and she used his distraction to roll his body underneath hers, her wolf demanding control. Lake let her have it. If he didn't, she'd never be able to overpower him and take Lake's control from him. He smiled up at her and God, he was so damn sexy.

"Move for me, Baby," he ordered. Star did as he asked and rode his cock and this time when she told him that she was going to come, he didn't stop her. Lake snaked his hand down between their bodies and stroked her clit, helping her to find her release. She shouted out his name, listening as it echoed back to his little pick-up truck parked on the side of the mountain. And, when Lake shouted her name into the cold night, it danced through the air, playing with her own screams. It was perfect, and Star finally felt like she had come home—not just to her childhood home, her reservation, and her little hometown, but to Lake Sani—the man who still owned her heart.

LAKE

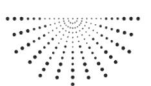

They spent another couple hours laying naked under the stars in the back of his pick-up and each passing minute had him hoping for yet another one. He dreaded the thought of having to take Star home, but he knew how important tomorrow was for her, starting her new job. So, they put their clothes back on and she helped him pull the tarp back over their makeshift little love nest, to head back into town.

"I had a really good time tonight," she said when they turned the corner to head back to her cabin. She had been so quiet for most of the ride home, he worried that he had done something wrong. He was careful not to push her too fast. Lake knew she had issues with being made to feel pressured and he wouldn't make that same mistake again. He pushed her ten years ago and that had her packing her shit and running away—far away. But, she was back again and even if his heart was considering her to be his, his brain knew better than to let his mouth speak those words out loud.

"Fuck," she swore when they pulled into her driveway. He parked his truck behind another black pick-up, and Star jumped down out of his truck, not waiting for him to get her door. She started for her cabin and that's when Lake saw the guy standing in the corner of her porch. "What are you doing here, Dane?" she growled.

"Good to see you too, Star," he said. "I told you what would happen if you chose not to come home. It's time to stop this ridiculous shit and come back home with me." He reached for her arm and she pulled it free. Lake watched the shot of anger cross her ex's face and he knew that he was holding back for Lake's benefit. He wondered if the asshole had ever hit her or Kai. But, he already knew the answer to his question from the way Star cowered as he towered over her tiny frame.

Dane looked him over as if finally acknowledging that Lake was standing there. "Who do we have here?" her ex asked.

"Lake Sani," he said. He crossed the small front yard and climbed onto the porch to stand next to Star, putting his arm around her.

Dane looked between the two of them and laughed. "So, this is him then?" he asked. Lake wasn't sure what Dane was talking about. He had a pretty good idea that Star had told him about Lake, and he wasn't too happy about finding them spending time together.

"Please Dane," she begged. Lake hated that she was begging her ex for anything. "Don't do this," she said.

Dane's laugh was mean, "You haven't told him yet then, have you?" he asked.

"Told me what?" Lake questioned.

"Can you just go in the house and make sure that Kai is safe?" she asked Lake. He knew she was trying to keep him out of their conversation but that just wasn't going to happen.

"And leave you out here with him? Not a chance," Lake growled.

"He's a shifter too, right?" Dane sounded like he was accusing him of something, rather than asking a question.

"That's none of your business," Lake spat. "Why are you here?" he asked her ex.

Dane barked out his laugh, "That's none of your business," he said, giving Lake back his words. "This here is a family discussion and you aren't my family," he said, motioning between him and Star. "When you planning on telling everyone, Honey?" Dane asked Star. She looked down at her hands, and he took a menacing step towards her. Lake hated the way Star seemed to cower next to him. He'd never let that asshole lay a hand on her. Lake stepped between Dane and Star, blocking her from her ex. "And, he plays the hero," Dane spat. "Good qualities to have in a mate and a baby daddy—right, Honey?" he asked.

"Baby daddy?" Lake asked. "I thought you were her husband, and not just Kai's dad." Star put her hand on Lake's forearm and he looked down at her, trying to put all the pieces together.

"I wanted to tell you, Lake. I'm so sorry. I was afraid, young, and stupid. I made the wrong decisions. I believed that letting Dane think he was Kai's father was the right decision." Lake pulled his arm free from her hand and took a step back from her.

"Yeah—now he's getting it. How does it feel to be lied to, man? I can tell you it hurts like hell to find out the truth. Here, I thought my sweet little wife was telling me the truth —that Kai was mine. Sure, I had my moments of doubt, but she swore he was my kid. I learned the hard way that she's a lying bitch. She took off, taking my kid with her, and left me with divorce papers as my parting gift."

"I didn't mean to lie to either of you," she whispered. Lake felt like his head was spinning, and he just wanted to get out of there. He stepped from the porch and headed for his truck.

"This is what happens when you're a lying bitch," Dane spat.

"Shut the fuck up and leave us alone," Star said. She turned to follow Lake from the porch, and before he could warn her, Dane spun her around and backhanded her jaw. Lake didn't think—he just reacted and was up on the porch, pinning Dane to the side of the cabin.

"You all right, Star?" Lake asked. She was holding her face and sobbing, and the sound nearly tore his damn heart out.

"I—I think so," she stuttered. Lake grabbed Dane by the collar of his jacket and let his inner wolf growl from deep within.

"You stay the fuck away from Star and Kai, asshole. I don't want you stepping foot on my reservation again or I'll have you thrown in jail," Lake promised.

"Someone die and leave you in charge?" Dane smirked at his joke.

"Actually, yeah," Lake said. Dane's smile quickly faded. "I'm chief around here, and if I hear that you stepped foot on my land, I'll have you tossed in jail. How will that look, Dane?" Lake asked. "I'm sure the media will have a field day with the whole thing. Big-time hockey player put in jail for trespassing."

"Fine," Dane spat. "I've done what I came here to do," he said. "She's all yours. Good luck with her." Dane shoved Lake back and pushed his way past him to step off the porch. "Later bitch," he said to Star over his shoulder. He was about to get into his truck when he stopped and looked back to where Star stood on her porch. "Oh—I'll sign your divorce papers, Honey. But, you and that brat won't see a dime from me. I'll see to that personally." Dane slipped into the driver's seat, started up his pick-up, and took off.

"I'm so sorry," Star sobbed. She stood by her front door and Lake looked into the window, to find Kai watching the whole scene, and the kid looked terrified. Was this his life back in Vancouver? How he had missed that Kai was his kid now baffled him. When Lake looked at him, he could see his eyes staring back at him, and the last thing he wanted to do was fuck things up with him. He wanted a chance to get to know his son.

"We have an audience," Lake whispered, nodding to the front window. He took Star's hand and pulled her along to his pick-up. At least they would have a little privacy there. They sat in silence for what felt like an eternity, Kai still watching from the front window.

"I never meant for you to find out that way," Star said. She was staring out the windshield at her son, and Lake could tell that she was trying to hold it together the best she could.

"Did you plan on ever telling me about my son?" he asked. He sounded meaner than he intended, but his world felt like it was spinning out of control. "What was the plan here, Star? Did you know this whole time that he's mine?" He hoped that her answer would be no—that she thought Kai was Dane's but only discovered recently that wasn't the case. It would be an easier pill to swallow if that was her story, but then she shook her head and Lake knew that he wasn't going to like what she said next.

"I knew," she admitted. He groaned and ran his hands through his unruly hair.

"How could you keep it from me? Does Kai know?" he asked. He had about a million other questions but overwhelming her wouldn't get him answers.

"No, he doesn't know, but I planned on telling him too," she said.

Lake barked out his laugh, "You lied to everyone and thought that telling the truth ten years later would what—just make everything okay? As if the truth could make up for all that lost time and wipe the slate clean?" He looked over at Star but she still refused to face him. She shrugged and wiped at the hot tears that spilled down her face.

"I was scared and stupid, Lake. I had just moved to the West Coast and met Dane. He didn't want anything serious and a relationship was the last thing I wanted. I was still in love with you," she whispered.

"Bullshit," he spat. "I told you that I loved you, Star, and you ran like hell to get away from me. If you were in love with me, why'd you take off?" he asked.

"Because you scared me, Lake. Like I said—I was scared and stupid. I didn't know what love could be between two people. I didn't have the best role models when it came to seeing two people in a loving relationship. When you told me that you loved me, I panicked and took off. I thought you'd be better off without me. I met Dane and he was a nice distraction at first." The last thing he wanted to do was sit in his truck and listen to Star talk about her sex life and the way Dane distracted her into forgetting about him. But, he wanted to know why she left and Star was finally talking to him. Sure, it had taken her ten years to do it, but he needed to hear her out.

"I found out that I was pregnant, about two months in, with Dane. At first, I thought the baby was his, never imagining that I was pregnant when I left here. But then, I had my first doctor's appointment and was measuring a little big for my timeline and well, that's when I found out that Kai was yours."

"And, you didn't think about at least calling me to tell me that I was going to be a father, Star? I would have taken care of you and our son," he said.

"I know that and maybe that's part of the reason I didn't call you, Lake. The thought of coming back here, and becoming my mother, scared the shit out of me. I didn't want to be stuck on the reservation in a no end relationship. I didn't want to end up hating you because I felt trapped or worse—you hate me because I had trapped you." It hurt that Star equated being with him as feeling trapped.

"Is that what being with me makes you feel like, Star?" he whispered. "Like you're trapped? Why agree to go on a date with me tonight if that's how you feel?" he asked.

"It's how I used to feel," she said. "I was so young and naive, Lake. I thought I was doing the right thing for both of us."

"And what about Kai, Star?" he asked. "Was it the best for him not to know that I'm his father? Was it best for him to grow up with a man like Dane as his dad? A man who beat you?" He guessed that last part, but after watching the two of them together tonight, he had a pretty good idea that his accusations were correct.

"No," she said, "it wasn't best for Kai, and I realized that over time. It's why we ended up leaving. Dane wasn't always abusive," she said. Hearing her defend that asshole felt like a punch to the gut. "He just assumed that Kai was his, and I let him. But then, when Kai was born two months earlier than his supposed due date, he started asking questions. I think that a part of him knew that Kai wasn't his and well, that's when his true nature started to poke its ugly head out. I started seeing the nasty, dark side of him. He'd come home drunk after a game, smelling like other women, and I knew what was happening. I was in so deep, getting out of that life didn't feel like a possibility. I thought that uprooting Kai would be a mistake, so I turned the other cheek and ignored his bad behavior. That's when he started hitting me," she whispered.

"How long did that go on?" Lake asked.

"Years," she sobbed, covering her face with her hands as if trying to hide from him. "I'm so ashamed that I let it go on for so long but I did. Every time it happened, he always felt so bad the next day. He'd swear that it would never happen again and God—I was a fool and believed him."

"Why now?" Lake asked. "Why after all these years did you finally decide that enough was enough?"

"He hit Kai," she said. "I couldn't stay with him anymore when he hit my son."

"Our son," Lake shouted. "He hit our son and I'm going to fucking kill him." Star cringed and cowered close to her door. He could tell that he had frightened her and seeing her reaction made him instantly regret his anger. He'd never lay a hand on her or any woman, for that matter. Cowards beat women and Dane was just that. "I want visitations with Kai," he whispered, trying to calm down. Sitting in his truck and yelling at Star wasn't going to change the past. The only way forward was to work out a future that involved him being able to get to know his child.

"Of course," she agreed. "That was part of the reason I came back here—for you and Kai to get to know each other. I just hope that you'll give me a day or two to tell him. He'll need time to adjust to the news, Lake. I won't rush him or push him into something he's not ready for, just to fix things. This is my mistake and I don't want to mess Kai up any more than I already have. I'll sit him down and talk to him."

"I'd like to be there when you do," he said. "I think I have a right to be there when you tell him I'm his father. I want Kai to know that he's important to me." Lake knew he was asking a lot, but Star owed him at least that.

"All right," she agreed.

"What was the other reason you came back?" he asked.

"Sorry?" she questioned.

"You just said that one of the reasons you came back home was so that Kai and I could get to know each other. What were the other reasons?" he asked.

Star stared out at her cabin again and when she didn't make a move to answer him, he wondered if she was going to. "To see you," she whispered. "I still had feelings for you, Lake," she admitted. "Hell, I think I'm still in love with you—not that you want to hear that right now."

"No," he barked. Star jumped, startled by his shouting. "I don't want to hear that from you, Star. You lied to me and that's something I don't think I'll be able to ever work past. I think it would be best for Kai if whatever happened between us tonight, just be forgotten." As if he could forget making her his again after ten years of pining for her. He had dreamed of a night, just like tonight, for so long now. He never stopped loving her but that wasn't something he'd admit to. He had enough lies from his father, not telling him about his sisters and past life with their mother, before finding his mother and making a life with her. He had forgiven his father but this was a whole different level of deceit. Star had kept his son from him for the first nine and a half years of his life. Lake had missed so much time with his son—time he'd never be able to replace, and that was unforgivable.

"Lake," she sobbed.

"Please don't, Star. I'll call you in the morning to set up a time to come over, so we can sit down with Kai, and tell him the truth. Then, you and I can come up with a visitation schedule. When Kai's comfortable with me, I'd like for him to start spending some nights over at my place. I want to be his father," Lake whispered. Star wiped at her tears and nodded. "Please send Ash out. I'll run him home. I've already paid him for the night," he said.

Star didn't say another word to him, just got out of his truck and walked up to her porch. Lake watched as she disappeared into her house and then Ash came out, taking Star's place in the front passenger seat. "What the hell was that?" Ash asked.

"You know your mother hates when you talk like that, Ash," Lake said. The teen shrugged.

"I'm almost an adult," he defended. "Just a few more months and I'll be eighteen," Lake remembered being eighteen and carefree. How had his life become so fucked up in just a few days? First, he lost his mother and his father had seemed to fall off the face of the damn planet. Then, the only woman he'd ever loved, walked back into his life and threw him the biggest curveball he'd ever had. Fucked up didn't even begin to describe his life these past few days.

"Don't be in such a hurry to grow up, kid," Lake grumbled. "Being an adult isn't all it's cracked up to be."

STARDUST

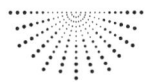

Star barely slept most of the night. She had questions to answer from her very upset son and when he finally accepted that Dane wasn't coming back, that he'd never be able to hurt them again, and that they were safe, he settled down to sleep. He had seen the whole ugly mess between Dane, Lake, and her on the front porch. Her only saving grace was that he couldn't hear what was being said from where he watched from, inside the cabin. He still didn't know that Lake was his dad and that the man who she allowed to hurt them all these years, was just a shitty choice she made for them both. Her son would find that out tonight though because Lake had texted her at the crack of dawn, to let her know he'd be over tonight at seven to talk to Kai.

Time was not on her side, and the panic she felt in the pit of her stomach kept her up all night. She finished up packing and at least could call her and Kai "settled in", even though she felt anything but settled. Kai got up and ready for school.

He seemed pretty excited about going and she was glad about that. He couldn't stop talking about his classmates and the fact that they were all shifters just like him. She loved that he finally felt like he fit in. Star felt the same way being back home, but she wondered how long it would take for people to find out the truth about what she had done to their chief and turn on her. It would happen—gossip spread like wildfire in their tiny town and soon, she'd be at the top of the chain. Star had a pretty thick skin, but she worried about her new job, and how it would be impacted, once the truth came out about her keeping Lake from his son. All she wanted was to make a life for herself on the reservation and to do that, she needed a job to put food on the table and keep clothes on her son's ever-growing back.

She and Kai got to school early since they were both excited to start their days. Honestly, she was more nervous than excited, but she wasn't about to tell her son that. Kai always seemed to carry her burdens on his shoulders. It was time she stopped letting him do that. He needed to be a kid for as long as possible and here, back in her little hometown, she could give that to him.

"Can I go in by myself?" Kai asked.

"You don't want me to walk you to class?" she questioned. Star knew this day would come—her son was going to start pushing her out of his life, claiming his independence, and that sucked. She loved that he felt confident to do it, especially with last night's little setback, but it still hurt that he was effectively dismissing her and the fact that he didn't need her to coddle him anymore.

"All right," she said when he shook his head. "Have a great

day, Kai," she said. She leaned over to let him kiss her cheek, just as she did every morning, and her son sighed, rolled his eyes, and gave her a quick, obligatory peck on the cheek.

"Bye, Mom," he shouted back over his shoulder as he quickly got out of her truck. She watched as he ran into the school and couldn't decide if his new show of independence made her want to laugh or cry. There was no time for crying and she had done enough of that all night long. Star pulled her brown paper bag lunch from the back seat and grabbed her purse. It was time to start a new chapter in her life and put her best foot forward, as her mother used to say.

She was just about to the school when she spotted Kaiah. Star foolishly pretended that she didn't see Lake's sister and her brood of noisy kids. Kaiah had her hands full and missing the noisy bunch would be damn near impossible. "We're pretty hard to miss," Kaiah shouted over her fussy baby. Star sighed, knowing that she had been found out, she turned to face Lake's older sister and every ounce of her judgment.

"I'm sorry," Star said. "I'm just in a hurry—first day and all." Star held up her brown paper bagged lunch, as if that were enough to prove that she was starting her first day as the school librarian.

Kaiah giggled, "Good choice in the packed lunch. Cafeteria food here isn't the best." She made a face and Star couldn't help her smile. Kaiah was being nice to her, and she wondered what that was all about.

"Lake told you," she said, squinting her eyes at his sister. That would explain the complete one-eighty in the way Kaiah was treating her.

"Yeah," Kaiah breathed. She bent and kissed each of her kid's cheeks and told them all to behave and make good choices, as they ran into the school together. Kaiah switched the baby to her other hip and focused on Star again. "You did the right thing by telling him, Star."

"Sure," Star spat. "I was just ten years late in doing it," she said. "Listen, I'm not defending myself here. Believe me, I feel awful for keeping Lake from his son, but I thought I was doing the right thing. I was wrong and I'm here to fix things."

"I believe you, Star. I know you mean well, but you have to understand that Lake is hurting right now. He's going to need time to heal. He feels like you betrayed him," Kaiah said.

"He's right to feel that way," Star said. "I did betray him and the whole town will find out what I did. Everyone will hate me and they have every right to. I did an awful thing keeping Kai and Lake apart all these years. If I could go back and time to fix it, I would—but I can't."

"Not everyone in town will hate you, Star," Kaiah said, reaching for her free hand. "I might have come off as a hard-ass before but it was just because I was looking out for my brother. I didn't meet him until we were both adults because our father chose to keep his secrets. I just didn't want that for Kai. Lake's dealing with a lot right now," she defended. "He just lost his mom, our father is MIA and now, you show back up in town and turn him inside out." Pictures of just how inside out Lake had turned her the night before flashed through her mind and Kaiah dropped her hand. "Sorry," she said. "TMI," Kaiah teased.

"Well, it wouldn't be too much information if you stayed out of people's heads," Star countered.

Kaiah giggled, "Where would the fun be in that?" she asked. "Listen, I just wanted to let you know that I'm in your corner—even when things seem to be at their worst, you can always come to me."

Star nodded, "I appreciate that Kaiah. Thank you," she said.

"Will I get to meet my nephew—you know officially as his auntie?" she asked. Kai had grown up with no cousins, aunts, or uncles. Dane and Star both were only children, and she was happy that her son would have all of that now, with Lake's family.

"Of course," Star agreed. "Just give Lake and me some time to explain everything to Kai. We're telling him tonight."

"Well, you just let me know when it's safe to dote on my new nephew," Kaiah said. "My kids are going to have so much fun with their new cousin." Kaiah's pack was a little overwhelming, but she knew that Kai would feel the same way about his new cousins.

"Thanks, Kaiah," Star whispered. The bell rang and she cursed.

"Shit," she whispered. "I'm officially late for my first day."

"Oh—yeah," Kaiah said. "Sorry, you go and good luck today and tonight telling Kai," she said.

Star ran into the school's front office. She smiled at the same secretary who used to give her hell for playing hooky back in the day. The woman seemed less than enthusiastic about being at work.

"I'm Stardust Luntz and I'm here for my first day, as the new librarian," she said.

"Yes, I remember you, Star," she said. "I'll buzz you back

and you're to go straight to the library." Star nodded and pulled the door open to the main office that led back into the school. She quickly found her way back to the library that sat between the gymnasium and the cafeteria—a layout that she always found odd. When she was a kid going to school there, she'd sit in the library—her favorite place in the whole school and read while listening to balls bouncing off the walls of the gym and smelling peanut butter and jelly sandwiches from the cafeteria. That was back in the good old days when peanut butter was allowed in school and dodgeball wasn't considered too dangerous to be played.

Star found her way back to the circulation desk and found Mrs. Hayward standing behind the desk waiting for her along with Lake. Star could feel her smile turn into a frown, as soon as she spotted him, and she tried to recover. Why wouldn't he tell her that he would be seeing her this morning? Unless this was an ambush that he planned after their disastrous date to sabotage her first day.

"Hello," Star croaked, clearing her throat. "I'm sorry I'm a few minutes late. First day jitters and all," she lied. There would be no way that she'd admit to being late because she was having a conversation with Lake's sister in the parking lot. She didn't want Lake to think that she was running around town trying to get people on her side.

"Things don't usually get busy back here before second period," Mrs. Hayward said. "It's good to see you, Star." Star smiled and nodded. "Mr. Sani usually helps me to welcome the new staff here at the school—you know in an official capacity. He's also shared the good news about you both sharing custody of Kai." Shit—that was exactly what she didn't need her first day at her new job, Lake running around telling everyone his side of things before she had a chance to sit Kai down to explain things to him.

"I hope that Mr. Sani has also told you how important it is that we keep this news private until we have a chance to talk to Kai. He doesn't know that Lake is his father yet, and we hope he doesn't hear the news around school before we can sit down together tonight to tell him." She shot Lake a look letting him know that she wasn't pleased that he was sharing news about her with others. What was happening between the three of them was private and should be kept between her, Kai, and Lake.

"I assure you that I've only shared our news with Mrs. Hayward and she's promised not to tell Kai's teachers until she's gotten the all-clear from both of us," Lake said. He smiled but it didn't reach his eyes. He seemed barely able to look at her, and Star wondered if they'd ever find their way back to being friends again. He just found out that he had a kid out in the world that he didn't know about. Star knew that she needed to cut him some slack but the way Lake treated her—so cold and distant, was hurtful.

"I appreciate that, Mrs. Hayward," Star said.

"I'm assuming that the man listed on Kai's birth certificate, Mr. Dane Michaels, should be taken off of your son's records?" she asked. This wasn't something that Star felt comfortable talking about with her old teacher, but she also knew it was inevitable.

"I will be removing Mr. Michaels as Kai's biological father, as soon as I have the funds to do so," Star said. "I'm in the process of divorcing Dane, and he now knows that Kai isn't his son. He won't contest it, but there will be fees associated with updating his records and legally changing his name. I will turn them into the front office as soon as I have everything in order," Star said.

"I'll pay for it," Lake offered. "He's my son and the sooner I get that ass—" Mrs. Hayward cleared her throat and Lake stopped talking. "Sorry, Mrs. Hayward. I forgot where I am. What I meant to say is the sooner I can get Mr. Michaels," Lake said through his clenched teeth, "out of my son's life, the better."

"Well, I think that it's time for me to head back to my office to get my day started. Mrs. Barber will be in to help you in about thirty minutes, at the start of second period, Star. She's been running the library for us until we could find a permanent replacement. She's going to be so happy you're here—her maternity leave should start any day now. Mrs. Barber will be training you over the next few days, to make sure that you're comfortable with everything. Please feel free to ask me if you have any questions." Mrs. Hayward left the library, leaving Star alone with Lake. The library suddenly felt a whole lot smaller with the way he stared her down.

"I see that you've taken the night to move into the next phase of hating me," she said. Star found a small, unused shelf under the circulation desk and stowed her things on it. "I don't expect your forgiveness, Lake. But, if you and I are going to co-parent Kai, we need to at least be civil towards each other. He's been through enough with Dane, he doesn't deserve your anger."

Lake took a step back from her as if she had slapped him. "I'd never be angry at Kai," he said.

"Good to know. Please reserve your anger towards me, for times like this—when we're alone. As far as Kai's concerned, everything is fine," she said.

"Got it—I'll pretend that you didn't hide my son away from me for almost ten years and keep us from having a relationship. Well, unless we're alone," he spat. Yeah—he was good and pissed. Taking the night to stew about the news didn't help matters, but his wounds were still so fresh, that she couldn't blame him for the way he was talking to her. "Anything else?" he asked.

"Can you please hold off on telling people about Kai?" she asked. Yeah—that wasn't a fair request but she worried that somehow things would get back to her son and she didn't want him to hear the news from strangers. Not that it would be any less of a blow coming from her and Lake tonight. "What happens if he hears the news from one of the kids in his class or worse—the staff whispering behind his back about you and me?"

"There is no you and me," Lake almost shouted. He looked around the room as if to make sure that they were still alone and back at her.

"I gathered that from your speech last night—you want a relationship with Kai and nothing to do with me. I'm fine with that, Lake," she lied. Her voice quivered from her trying to hold back the damn of emotions that she kept bottled up. It was taking everything in her not to break down, but that wasn't how she wanted her first day going.

"Good," Lake said. "I'll hold off on telling more people but you need to know that after we tell Kai tonight, I'm not going to stay silent about what happened with us, Star. I won't deny my son."

"No one is asking you to, Lake. I'm truly happy that you want a relationship with Kai. I'm a big girl and can handle the way people are going to talk about me, but we need to remember that Kai will hear those same rumors. How do you think it will make him feel hearing that his mother's a horrible person, and kept his father from him?" Her voice cracked again and this time she couldn't keep the tears at bay. "I won't do that to him, Lake. I won't stay here and let him be ashamed of me because of what other people are saying."

Panic flashed through Lake's eyes and he took a menacing step toward her. Her instincts kicked in and she stepped out of his path, covering her face with her arms, readying herself for the punch he was about to throw.

"Star," he whispered. Her eyes were squinched shut and she was too afraid to open them. "Star look at me. I'll never do that to you," he promised. "I'm not Dane and I'd never hit you or Kai." She squinted an eye open to find him standing back where he originally was, out of her reach. She nodded and lowered her hands from her face.

"Sorry," she whispered. "I guess it's just something that I expect now since—well, since Dane."

"I'm not him and I'd never lay a hand on you—either of you," Lake promised. "I'm sorry that happened to you, Star." It was the first time that Lake spoke to her with any compassion, since he found out the truth last night, and she counted it as a small win. "Maybe you could see someone to help you through this," he said.

"Like a shrink?" she asked.

Lake shrugged, "Sure, a doctor or therapist who can help you through everything Dane did to you. Might be a good idea for Kai, too. Hell, we could probably get a group rate and work through this new territory of co-parenting and shit." She cleared her throat at his use of curse words, just as Mrs. Hayward had and he laughed. "Yeah—maybe I should spend less time on school property," he said. "Just think about it. I'm sure I can find you both a good therapist who'd be able to help."

"I think that would be a good idea," she said. "As long as my new insurance covers it. Thanks, Lake." He nodded and started for the door.

"I'll be by your place tonight at seven," he said back over his shoulder. She nodded, knowing that he wouldn't be able to see her, but saying anything back without starting up again with the waterworks, wasn't going to happen. She needed to get through her first day of work and then, she'd worry about correcting her past mistakes. Somehow, she was going to get through this mess she made of her life and find a way to redeem herself with her son and the people in town—but most of all with Lake.

LAKE

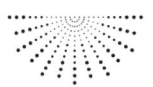

He threw himself into his work and even dug up the paperwork necessary to change Kai's last name, and have his name placed as Kai's biological father, on his birth certificate. Every time he thought about the red tape and hoops that he'd have to jump through to prove that he was Kai's father, he got angrier with Star. He knew she was trying to correct her past wrongs but all this shit could have been avoided if she had just come clean and told him the truth from the very beginning.

Instead, he had to call the lawyer, that he kept on retainer, and spill the whole sorted story over the phone to him. He had made Star a deal that he wouldn't tell anyone else until they sat Kai down and told him tonight, but he was anxious to get the ball rolling on making Kai his—legally. Besides, Tom was on retainer, and anything he said to him would be considered confidential information, and he knew that his old friend could keep his mouth shut.

At about noon, he gave up pretending to be productive and stuck his head into Zoe's office, to tell her that he was heading home early. He told her he wasn't feeling well, but when she shot him a look letting him know she had caught him in a lie, he slumped into the closest chair and kicked her door shut.

"You going to just tell me or do we have to sit here and play twenty questions?" Zoe asked.

Lake shot her a look and sighed, "I made a promise I'd keep my mouth shut until tomorrow."

"What's happening tomorrow?" Zoe asked. He looked at her again and this time when he dramatically sighed she pulled a pack of bubble gum from her drawer.

"Lake," she said, opening a piece of gum and shoving it into her mouth. "I'm your oldest and dearest friend," she said.

"You think way too highly of yourself," he mumbled. "But, you're right—you are my oldest friend, Zoe," he teased. He watched as she opened the foil wrapper around two new pieces of gum and shoved them into her mouth. That made three pieces and he knew exactly what game she was playing.

"And, as your dearest friend," she said around a mouth full of bubble gum, ignoring his slight of calling her old, "I know all the ways to get under your skin. Heck—I know all the ways to make your skin crawl if I wanted to be an ass," she said. She opened two more pieces and shoved them into the wad of gum that she had already begun chewing, and his stomach felt as though it was flip-flopping in protest.

"You are foul," he accused.

She laughed with her mouth wide open, exposing the soft

wad of chewed bubble gum inside. "You have no idea what I'm capable of or the lengths I'd go to figure out what's going on in that handsome head of yours, Lake." Oh—he had a pretty good idea what his best friend was capable of. She had been doing shit like this to him since they were kids. Zoe knew how much Lake hated gum. He hated chewing it—the texture of it in his mouth but more than that, he hated watching other people chew gum. And God, the sound of them chewing and popping the gum in their mouth, made him want to stab his eardrums just to escape it. Yep—Zoe was pure evil and she'd go to great lengths to get him to spill his guts.

She blew out a giant bubble as she stood from the other side of her desk, resting her ass on the corner, just in front of him. Lake watched her like a hawk because taking his eyes from her was always a giant fucking mistake. Zoe would wait for him to falter and then swoop in for the kill, or in this case, the chance to stick her soft, warm gum on him.

"Zoe," he said, in warning. "Stop being a child." Her smile was mean and he knew he was about to lose at their little game. "I swear, Zoe" he growled, skootching back in his chair as far as he could. "I'll fire your ass if I have to." Zoe reached into her mouth and pulled out the giant wad of gum, smiling down at him. It was like being back in grade school all over again but now, he knew Zoe well enough to know that she'd go through with whatever evil plan that was running through her brain if he didn't cooperate.

He stood and escaped to the far side of her office, cowering in the corner. "Don't be such a baby, Lake," she said. "You know what will happen if you don't tell me what's going on." She held up the lump of gum, waving it in the air, as a threat.

"Fine," he spat. "I'll tell you but throw that wad of shit away and wash your damn hands," he ordered. She smiled and did as he asked, and when she came out of the private bathroom that joined their two offices, he swore she said something smug and smart ass under her breath. Yeah—she won this time, but only because she played dirty.

"All clean," she said, holding up her hands as if providing him proof. She picked up the pack of gum she kept in her desk and shoved it back into the top drawer. "Spill it, or we start our little game over," she taunted.

"You know, if this gig as my assistant doesn't work out, you can go into torturing people for a living. You missed your calling in life, Zoe," he accused. Her laugh sounded evil and Zoe sat back in her chair, waiting him out. "I found out that Kai, Star's kid—well, he's my kid, too." He crossed the small office to sit back down in the chair he had just vacated.

"Wait—what?" she asked. "You and Star had a kid together?"

"Yep," he breathed.

"And, she kept that from you all these years?" Zoe asked.

"Yep," Lake said. "He's nine and a half and I didn't even know he existed until a few days ago. How's that for fucked up?"

"I'm going to need more details," she said. "How did you find out? Did she tell you? Wait—weren't you supposed to go on a date with her last night? Oh God—please don't tell me that she told you the news over dinner," she moaned.

"Are you done with the questions?" he asked. Zoe waved her hand at him like she wanted him to get on with it, and he smiled. "I did have a date with Star. I took a picnic dinner of her favorite subs up to The Bluffs, and we laid out under the stars."

"So, she didn't spill the beans over dinner?" Zoe asked.

"No," Lake breathed. "She waited until we had sex in the back of my pick-up and then when we got back to her cabin, her ex was waiting to fill me in on the details."

"No," Zoe breathed. "He was just there, waiting for you two to get back to her cabin? Wait—you two had sex?" Lake's head felt as though it was spinning from all her questions.

"How about you let me tell the story and then, I'll be happy to take any questions," Lake said, giving her his best, "chief in charge" voice, as she liked to call it.

"Fine," she said, sitting back in her chair again. He knew she didn't mean it and would be chiming in with more questions at any minute.

"Yes, we had sex and God—it was perfect. I guess it only drove home the fact that I'm not really over Star. Maybe I never was, but that doesn't matter now," he said.

"Well, why not?" Zoe asked. He shot her a look and she smirked, holding up her hands as if she was willingly backing down. "Sorry, won't happen again," she lied.

"It doesn't matter now because Star lied to me. All these years, she kept my kid from me, and that's just unforgivable," he said.

"The only unforgivable things in life is stuff you aren't willing to let go of, Lake. Everything is forgivable if you're willing to let your heart accept it and move on," Zoe said. He hated it when she made sense. He hated it even more when she was right.

"Well, this is pretty unforgivable. I don't think I can let Star into my heart or life again," he said.

"But, you'll have no choice in the matter, Lake. If Kai's your kid, you'll have to deal with her as his mom. You sure he's your son?" Zoe asked. Tom had asked him the same thing earlier. Telling his lawyer that the kid has his eyes, apparently wasn't the right answer. Tom ordered a DNA test that would give them conclusive results, that would hold up in a court of law, if necessary.

"He has my eyes," Lake said. Zoe nodded and smiled. That was enough reason to believe that Kai was his. He knew his best friend would understand that he just looked at the kid, after hearing the truth, and knew Kai was his son.

"So, why have you been sworn to secrecy by Star then?" Zoe asked.

"Her ex told me about Kai and then went after Star. The asshole's been beating the shit out of her all these years. She said that when he hit Kai, she packed their shit and left to come here. Well, he tracked her down after finding out where she was, and I had to tell him to stay clear of the reservation," Lake said.

"Of course you did," Zoe said.

"What the hell does that mean?" he asked.

"It means that you're a nice guy, Lake. No matter what Star has done to you—keeping your only son from you for ten years, you still helped her. You stood up to her bully of an ex because you're a nice guy," Zoe said.

"Stop saying that like it's a bad thing," he said. Lake would stand up for any woman in the same situation. Men who hit women were disgusting and he wouldn't allow it on his reservation—not while he was chief.

"It's not a bad thing. It's probably why you agreed to do the right thing and not tell anyone until you guys can sit down and tell Kai," she assumed.

"Damn—you're like a witch sometimes, Zoe," he said. "I mean—my sisters are gifted with sight. You sure you don't have the same abilities?"

"Nope," she said. "I just know you, Lake."

"The kid has the right to a normal life now, Zoe," Lake said. "If I can give that to him, I will."

"What happens when this thing gets out, and people around the reservation find out that Star kept Kai from you all these years?" she asked. He hadn't given that much thought before his little meeting with Star this morning. He thought about skipping the whole meet and greet with the new staff member, knowing that it was Star and seeing her again so soon after their disastrous date, didn't feel like such a great idea. But, he also knew that shirking his duties as chief wasn't who he was, and neither was running from his problems. He'd have to face down Star sooner or later and avoiding her wasn't going to work. Still, word was going to get around town and when it did, people would blame Star for keeping him from Kai. No matter how he would spin the story, they would find her to be the bad guy in the situation, that had nothing to do with them. Kai would pay the price, along with his mother. His son would hear the whispers and rumors and that wasn't the way he wanted his kid to grow up.

"No clue," Lake grumbled. "I'll figure something out though."

Zoe nodded, "You always do, Boss," she said. "It's who you are, Lake—the good guy."

He got to Star's cabin just before seven and parked in her gravel driveway. He looked into her lit up cabin and saw her in the kitchen doing dishes. He hated the worry that was etched in her beautiful face. Lake wasn't sure he'd ever be able to get past her lying to him, but that didn't stop him from loving her. She hurt him and he felt betrayed, but his damn heart still beat for her, just as it had for over ten years now. He wished there was a way to turn off his feelings but there wasn't. So, for now, he'd hang onto his anger, and hope that was enough for him to keep his damn hands to himself around her. Every time she cried or showed any vulnerability, he wanted to pull her against his body and promise that it was all going to be all right, but that would be a lie.

After he knocked off early from work, he shifted and went for a long run. It had been a long damn time since his wolf ran the entire reservation, but he did today. He was bone-tired and ready to call it a night, but he also was excited to tell Kai what he hoped his son would consider to be good news. Then, he needed to figure out how to tell the townspeople that he had a son without them lashing out at

Star and blaming her for keeping Kai from him. He felt that same anger but he didn't want it to affect Kai. He wouldn't let that happen.

He knocked on the front door and Kai opened it, all smiles, as he waved him into the house. "Mom said you were coming over to see me, Lake," Kai said. "Are we going to have pizza and watch a movie again?"

Star stood in the doorway to the kitchen drying her hands on a dishtowel. "You already had dinner, Son," she chided. "As for the movie—you have school tomorrow and if I'm not mistaken, you have homework to do still."

"Aw, Mom," Kai groaned.

"I won't be able to stay for a movie tonight anyway, Kai," Lake said. "I have work tomorrow and don't tell anyone but, I have some homework to finish up tonight too," he whispered that last part, causing Kai to giggle.

"You can't have homework—you're not in school," Kai challenged.

Lake laughed," Well, it's work and I have to do it from home, so it counts, right?" Kai shrugged and sat down on the sofa.

"Then, why'd you come over?" Kai asked.

"Kai," Star said. "Manners."

"Sorry," he mumbled.

"I came over because your mom and I have something we need to talk to you about," Lake said. Star tossed the dishtowel back onto the kitchen counter and sat down next to Kai. Lake sat down in the recliner, wanting to give them both some space. He knew from experience that what they were about to tell Kai was going to take him a few minutes to understand. When his dad told him about Kaiah and Aylen being his older sisters, he felt confused and angry. His dad was smart enough to give him some space and he could do the same for Kai.

"Are you getting married?" Kai asked his mom.

"Getting married?" she asked. "Why would you think that?"

Kai shrugged, "One of the kids in my class said that his mom thinks that you and Lake will probably get married, now that we're here in town. He said that's why you went on a date last night—to see if you still want to get married."

"Oh God," Star said, raising her shaking hand to her mouth. "It's only the beginning of what's going to be spreading around here." Lake could hear the panic in her voice—see it in her eyes and he hated how this was going to affect her and Kai. But, this mess was of her own making and Star was going to have to face the truth now.

"Did I say something wrong?" Kai asked.

"No," Lake breathed. "Your mom and I did go on a date last night but we aren't getting married. It was just to catch up and well, your mom had some really good news to tell me."

"News?" Kai asked. Lake looked at Star who still seemed pretty shaken up. He didn't want to be the one to tell Kai their news—that was something he promised her she could do. She nodded and wrapped a protective arm around Kai's small body.

"Yep—I did have some news to share with Lake. It's about you, son," she said.

"Me?" he questioned.

"Yes," Star paused and cleared her throat as if the next words she was about to say were nearly impossible for her to get out.

"Lake is your dad, Kai," she whispered.

"I have a dad," Kai challenged. "Dane's my dad. I call him dad," he said as if that was all the explanation she needed.

"I know son, but it's true. You see, Lake and I used to live together—here in this house. Well, when I left to move to Vancouver, I didn't know that you were in my tummy, and that's about the same time I met Dane."

"Were you married to Lake before?" Kai asked, interrupting her story.

"Before?" Lake asked.

"Yeah—when you lived here with mom, were you married then?" Kai asked. Lake looked at Star as if silently asking for guidance as to how to answer her. She shrugged, letting him know she was just as clueless in all this as he was.

"No," Lake breathed. "We were never married, but I loved your mom very much," he admitted. He wanted his son to know that he wasn't a mistake. He was conceived in love and if Star had just stayed in town, he would have asked her to marry him.

"Do you still love my mom?" Kai asked.

Star shook her head, "That doesn't matter now," she protested. "What matters is that we loved each other when we made you, Honey," she said.

"Yes," Lake admitted. "I still love your mom," he whispered.

"Oh," Star breathed. "You do?" Lake nodded and looked at

her—God, she made his heart flutter like a lovesick boy, but that wasn't what any of them needed now. He needed to hold onto what was important and that was getting Kai through this without fucking him up too much. Then, he'd deal with his messed up feelings for Star.

Lake nodded and looked back at Kai who was watching them both. "But, your mom and I have decided that we shouldn't see each other right now because I need to concentrate on getting to know you. Will you let me do that, Kai? Will you let me get to know you?" Lake watched his son's face as indecision played through his emotions. He was so much like Star—Lake could tell just what Kai was thinking by his expressions.

Kai stood and turned to face his mother. "You told me Dane is my dad," he said. "Lake can't be my dad because then you're a liar," he challenged. "You said it's bad to lie, Mom." Star stood and reached for Kai and he pushed her back down to the sofa.

"Kai," Lake shouted his name. "You cannot push your mother that way."

"I don't have to listen to you," he spat. "You're not my dad."

Lake towered over his son, "I am your dad, and like it or not, that's not going to change."

"I don't like it," Kai shouted. He slipped past Lake and ran out the front door and into the night.

"Kai," Star shouted. "Kai Michaels, you come back here right now." Lake ran out onto the front porch and watched as his son stripped out of his shirt and ran off into the woods. He shifted into his wolf form and took off.

"I need to go after him," Star said, pulling her shirt over her head. "I can connect to him and find him."

"Only if he wants to be found," Lake said. "I hid out from both of my parents by blocking my thoughts and I'm pretty sure Kai's smart enough to figure that out for himself. Just give him some time. This was a lot for him to accept."

"You don't get to tell me how to raise my kid, Lake," she challenged.

"Our kid and I'm pretty sure that is my job as his dad. I won't tell you how to raise him but I will tell you how I feel about how we raise him—together. Kai just needs some time and space," he said.

"Well, like father like son," Star challenged. "I guess that you know best now, right Lake?"

"What the hell does that mean?" he spat.

"It means that I wanted to ease into telling him and not just throw it in his face that you're his father. How do you think it made him feel to find out that he had been lied to his whole life?" she asked. Lake knew exactly how it felt to be lied to—first, by his father and now, by Stardust.

"I have a feeling I know how that feels," he said. He looked her over as if challenging him to tell him otherwise. She backed down and he did the same.

"He thinks I'm a liar now," she sobbed. "Everyone will think that and they're right—Kai's right. I can't make this right even if I want to now." Lake couldn't stand it anymore —watching Star cry always tore him apart. He had to move from his anger to find some forgiveness for the woman who was once his whole world. She was the mother of his son and lashing out at her was only hurting them both. Lake pulled her into his arms and she sobbed against his chest. "I'm so sorry," she whispered.

"I know," he said. He held her and let her cry. They stood like that, her whispering how sorry she was, and him silently letting go of the anger that consumed him for so long now. Anger over her walking away from him ten years ago, and anger for Star keeping Kai from him for so long. He let it all go and damn it—Zoe was right, he felt better.

"Shit," he spat.

"What's wrong?" Star asked.

"Zoe was right about something and that just pisses me off," he said. Star giggled and sniffled, wiping her face on his t-shirt.

"What about?" she asked.

Lake sighed, "She told me that I needed to forgive you to free myself from my anger. Said I had to do it not just for myself but for you and Kai."

"Wait—you're not angry with me?" she whispered.

"I'm getting there. It's a work in progress," he grumbled. "Let's go back in the cabin and wait for Kai. We need to talk a few things out and I'm sure that once he calms down, he'll be back. I used to run off into the woods all the time when I was his age." Star looked to the forest and back at him, nodding her agreement.

"What do we need to talk about?" she nervously asked.

"I think I have a way to work around the problem of everyone in town badmouthing you," he said. "It's a little crazy, but it just might work." His plan was a whole lot crazy but if it worked, she'd be spared embarrassment around town, and Kai wouldn't have to hear anymore whispered rumors about his mother and him. All he had to do was get Star on board and then they could put everything into action in the morning.

STARDUST

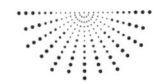

Lake was down on one knee, holding up his mother's wedding ring to her, and Star wasn't sure what the hell was going on. They were supposed to talk while they waited for Kai to blow off some steam, but as soon as she walked into her family room, she turned around to find Lake on his knees. "What the hell are you doing?" she asked.

"I'm fixing your problem," he said. "Marry me." He wasn't asking her a question-more like making a demand.

"You want me to marry you to fix my problem?" she questioned. He wasn't making any sense.

"Yep," he said. He was still down on his knee and she pulled on his arm to get him up, although that was like trying to move a brick wall.

"Please just get up, Lake," she insisted, still tugging on his arm. "I can't talk to you like this."

"Fine," he said. Lake stood from the wood floor and

crossed her small family room to sit on the sofa. "Listen, Star. I know it's not perfect but at least it's a plan."

"How is marrying you a plan, Lake?" she asked.

"Well," he said, clearing his throat and pulling her down to sit next to him. "We're going to have to tell everyone in town that I'm Kai's father. They're going to put two and two together and come up with something close to four." He smiled at her but she didn't feel much like laughing at his corny jokes. Right now, she was just trying to keep up with his train of thought.

"Right and I told you that my only concern is Kai. We need to try to shield him from the gossip train that will run through town," she said. She knew how cruel people could be and the last thing she wanted was for her son to get hurt by all the chatter.

"Understood," Lake said. "But, we just saw tonight that it will prove impossible to shield him from the gossip. You heard Kai—kids in class are talking about what they had heard at home. They told him that we're getting married."

"That does not mean that we need to do it," she objected. "Just because the crazy locals come up with false stories about us, doesn't mean that we have to make them true."

"I agree but Kai telling us about what the kids were saying gave me the idea. I mean, if people in town think that I'm okay with everything—that we're getting married, it will take away some of the gossip that's sure to circulate."

"Say I agree to this crazy scheme of yours," she said.

"Good, it's settled then," he said.

"No, it's not, Lake. I'm hypothetically speaking—you know, trying to work this all out in my mind." Lake sat back and sighed. "What are we going to tell everyone about Kai?"

"How about we tell them the truth but put a spin on it. We can tell them that I knew about him the whole time and that I was seeing him whenever I could get to the West Coast. That you and I had an arrangement when it came to me seeing Kai, and we thought it was best he didn't know about me until it was time," Lake said. His story would completely help her save face but throw himself under the bus, so to speak.

"The people in town will hate you instead of me," she whispered. "That's not fair to you, Lake."

"How about you let me worry about me," he said. "I'm chief and they will forgive me a whole lot faster than they will you, Star. Trust me, it will work."

"Okay," she said. He seemed to get excited again and Star held up her hand to stop his early celebration. "I wasn't agreeing with your plan yet." Lake rolled his eyes and sat back again. "What's the story about me coming back here? Why the change of heart?"

"That's the easy part—we stick to the truth. Your marriage didn't work out and you decided to come home to let me help with our son," Lake said.

"Everyone will believe that—it's the truth. But, there's still one more problem," she said.

"Shoot," he said.

"I'm still married to Dane and I can't marry you," she reminded.

"That's the beauty of the plan. We won't get married," he said. "We'll get engaged. Give everyone the story we want them to know, not the gossip they try to spread, and when your divorce is final, we can break-up."

"Break-up?" she whispered. Her heart sank at the mention of him breaking up with her, but his proposal of marriage was a plan he came up with to help her. He didn't plan on following through with the actual wedding part, and why would he? She had gotten caught up in the fairy tale he was selling her and forgetting that Lake was angry with her. He didn't want to be a part of her life—he made that clear last night. He was doing all of this for Kai's sake and she needed to remember that before she got hurt by getting caught up in Lake's story of them living happily ever after.

"Yeah—you wanted a plan that would keep Kai out of the gossip and this is it. You'll be able to stay in town and I'll get to know Kai," he said.

"I wouldn't leave town, Lake," she promised. Sure, it would suck to have to deal with being the talk of the town but she'd get through it. But, would Kai?

"I thought that once before and was wrong," Lake said. "I don't want to chance you getting sick of all the chit chat and taking off with Kai again. I need the chance to get to know him, Star—please," he begged. "I know my plan will work and when it's all done, you and I will have saved our son some embarrassment, and hopefully find a way to work together."

"And, what will we tell people about our break-up? No one will believe that it just didn't work out, not with our history, and now the fact that we have a son together," she said. No one would believe that she'd just break up with Lake, even if she was foolish enough to do it once before.

"We can tell everyone that I cheated on you," Lake said.

"No," she said. "No one will believe that, Lake. You're too nice of a guy."

"Why the fuck does everyone think I'm a nice guy?" he grumbled.

Star barked out her laugh, "Because you are," she insisted. He was one of the best people she had ever known. It's what made this whole situation suck even more. Lake had never been anything but loving and sweet to her and she went and ruined his life, walking away from him and keeping Kai from knowing him. No one would ever believe that Lake had it in him to cheat on her. "You're the best person I know, Lake."

"Then let me help—accept my plan. Let's keep Kai out of the gossip and give everyone a chance to accept our news. That's all it's going to take, Star—promise," he said.

They could sit around all night and debate the pros and cons of Lake's plan but the facts were—she needed this plan to work. Otherwise, she'd be the talk of the town and that wasn't something she was willing to put her son through. "All right," she said. "I'll agree to your plan. I'll marry you, Lake," she said. Kai came running into the house, naked and looked between the two of them. Lake was slipping his mother's ring onto her finger just as her son burst through the front door.

"Where have you been?" she asked, standing from the sofa. Star grabbed the blanket off the back of the sofa and wrapped it around her son. Gray followed him into the house and nodded to her and Lake.

"Kaiah sent me out after him," he explained. "She saw

what happened and well, she didn't want you to worry about the pup, so I decided to tag along for his run."

Lake nodded at Gray, "Thanks, man," he said. "We appreciate that."

"Go easy on the kid," Gray said, resting his hand on Kai's shoulder. "He's got a lot going on and this isn't easy for him."

"Will do," Lake promised. "We only want what's best for you, Kai," Lake said. His son stared him down and he smiled at him. Yeah, probably not what the kid wanted or expected, but he was so darn cute when he twisted his face into an angry scowl.

"And, Kai," Gray said, crouching in front of him. "Remember what we talked about. Adults make mistakes too and your mom and Lake deserve a chance to make things right. Give them a chance, Kai," Gray said.

"All right," Kai grumbled.

"Good, now go shower up," Gray ordered. Kai nodded and rand down the hall to the back bedrooms.

"Thank you," Star said. "I appreciate your help with him."

"We both do," Lake said.

"Not a problem," Gray said. "I've got to get back to Kaiah and the kids. It's my night to help with baths and she'll kick my ass if I'm late." Gray turned to leave and then looked back to Lake. "Oh, and your sister wanted me to tell you that it's a good plan, but you're an idiot." Gray chuckled and left.

"Why am I an idiot now?" Lake grumbled. Star was pretty sure she knew exactly why Kaiah had given her husband that message for her brother. She must have seen Star's disappointment when Lake told her the part about breaking up with her when it came time to follow through with the wedding part of his plan.

Kai came back to the family room, his hair wet, and in his pajamas. "You use soap?" Star questioned.

Kai rolled his eyes and nodded. "Yes, mom," he said. "Mr. Gray said that I should tell you that I'm sorry about running away," he said.

"Well, that's nice but I don't want you to say that unless you truly are, Son," she said. "Telling someone that you're sorry should come from the heart. If you don't mean it, it doesn't count," Star explained.

"I know," Kai said. "And, I mean it mom. I'm sorry that I ran off. I was a little bit afraid out in the woods by myself. I like Mr. Gray," he said.

Lake chuckled, "Everyone likes Gray," he said. "He's a nice guy and technically, he's your uncle."

"He told me that I have lots of cousins to play with," Kai said. "Is that true?" he asked Lake.

"Yes," Lake breathed. "I have two sisters that I didn't know until we were all adults," Lake said. "They both have lots of kids. You'll have a ton of playmates."

"I think I'd like that," Kai said. "Can I have a playdate, Mom?" he asked.

"Sure, Honey. I'll set something up with your Aunt Kaiah. You ready for bed?" she asked.

"Will Lake be spending the night?" he asked.

"Um—no," she said.

"But, when I came home, you said you'd marry him," Kai said. She could see the confusion on her son's face and she hated that things were so complicated.

"Your mom agreed to marry me, Kai," Lake said. She wanted to tell him that it was all fake—that she agreed to Lake's plan to keep her name out of the gossip mills, but she wasn't sure her son would understand. And, how would she explain the break-up to Kai, when it came time for that part of Lake's plan? She just needed to remember that her son was strong and that he had already gotten through her break-up with Dane, he'd find a way through the one with Lake, when it happened.

"Your mom has agreed to marry me but we're going to take things slowly, Kai," Lake promised. "That way you can get used to all of this. Does that work for you?" Lake asked. Kai seemed to be thinking it over and Star felt as though she was holding her breath waiting for him to answer. Kai finally nodded and she blew out her breath.

"Can Lake read me a story?" Kai asked. Star looked at him as if silently telling him it was his decision.

"I'd love to," Lake said. "Thanks, for asking, Kai," he said.

"I'll give you two some time and finish cleaning the kitchen from dinner," she offered. Star was going to have to get used to giving Lake and Kai some alone time to get to know each other. And, when they broke-up from their fake marriage proposal, she was afraid that she was going to have a whole lot more alone time—whether she liked it or not.

LAKE

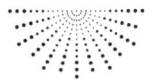

Their plan was working, for the most part. It had been almost a month since he and Star sat Kai down to tell him the truth. The next day, he was surprised to hear some of the rumors already circulating about them, but when he announced that he and Star were engaged, everyone seemed to buy it.

He and Star had worked out a nice rhythm of him stopping by her place to pick up Kai and avoiding each other. It was easier to deal with his anger than Star. He thought he was letting his anger go—finding a new way forward with her. He wasn't lying when he admitted to Kai that he was in love with Star. He had loved her since the day he met her and he never stopped loving her just because she walked away from him. Even when news got back to town that Star had married a hockey player from the West Coast, he never stopped loving her. It hurt like hell to know that he wanted that life with her—marriage, a kid, the whole nine yards. But,

Star chose to leave him and marry Dane. And, when her new husband decided to beat her, she chose to stay and put Kai in danger. Lake didn't trust her—he couldn't. Not with all the shitty decisions she had made that affected not only herself but him and his son.

Instead, he found himself avoiding her, and making excuses as to why she wasn't with him and Kai when they were out around town. He'd take Kai for pizza and when his son and the locals would ask where Star was, Lake would make some excuse for her, telling them that she wasn't feeling well or that she had some work to catch up on. But, she was at home, waiting for him to get back with Kai. Lake insisted that he needed time with his son. He convinced her that he and Kai needed some one-on-one time to get to know each other—that she owed that to him at the very least. He played on her never-ending guilt over what she had done—keeping Kai from him and though he knew it was a dick move, he didn't care.

The problem was, Lake wasn't sure he could forgive Star for what she had done. He wanted to, really he did, but his head wasn't willing to follow his heart. He loved her—that would never change because he didn't know how to make it stop. But, he worried that he'd never be able to completely forgive her, and if he couldn't do that, they would never have a future together. He knew that was what Star wanted. He could see it in her eyes every time he left her behind to take Kai out for some fun. He didn't miss the way she'd study his mother's ring on her finger when she thought he wasn't looking. She wished it was real—the whole ruse that he had concocted to protect Kai and ultimately, Star. If he was being honest, he wished it was real too but that would require him to find a way to forgive her. He was caught in a catch twenty-two and the only good thing he had going for himself right now was his relationship with Kai.

They were on their way to town to pick up a few office supplies that Zoe ordered and conveniently couldn't pick up. Her son had football practice and she was in charge of snacks for the team, which was a big deal. Instead, Lake picked Kai up after school because Star had a staff meeting she needed to attend, and it was his night with his son.

"Can we stop for pizza in town?" Kai asked. His son was always careful not to say his name. Before finding out that he was his father, he called Lake by his first name. But since then, he had never called him anything. Lake hoped that someday, Kai would call him "Dad," but he wouldn't push him into doing that—not until Kai was ready.

"We had pizza two nights ago," Lake challenged.

"I know but I love pizza," Kai said.

Lake chuckled, "Same son, same. But, I think I should do the adult thing and insist that we eat a meal that has a vegetable included." Kai grumbled something about him being worse than his mom, and Lake took that as a sign that he was doing something right as a parent. "It's just a salad," Lake teased. "I'm not asking you to give up pizza or anything."

"What if we got pasta with our salad," Kai said. "Would that count?"

"That counts," Lake agreed. "I just have to run by the office supply store and pick up my order, and then we can get some dinner. You want to eat at the restaurant or back at my place?" he asked. Kai shrugged and Lake could tell that his son had something that he wanted to say but he was holding back. "You know you can tell me anything, right?" Lake asked.

"Yeah," Kai said.

"I thought we had worked past all this awkward silence and me having to guess what you're thinking, Kai," Lake challenged.

"I just miss my mom," Kai whispered.

"You just saw her," Lake said.

"I know," Kai said. "She's always too busy to hang out with us. When you guys get married, are we going to live in different houses still?" His son was so smart, he had to have picked up that things weren't just as Lake had portrayed them to be. He and Star had been careful not to let Kai know that they were pretending to be a happy couple. They were always watching to make sure that they were alone before discussing what their next step was. He hated that they had to lie to Kai, but it was the only way to keep up the rouse. Plus, he didn't want to involve Kai in their crazy scheme. The less he knew the better. Lake's dilemma wasn't whether or not to tell Kai the truth, it was when, and that wasn't his decision to make alone. He was going to have to include Star in this, like it or not.

"How about we get our pasta and salad to go and take it back to your mom's house? I'm sure that she'll be hungry and will love it if we surprised her with dinner," Lake said. He knew that Star hated surprises but he had no other choice. He wouldn't be able to answer Kai's questions on his own and he had a feeling that his son wasn't going to give up asking them. "Plus—you're mom will help answer your questions," Lake said.

"All right," Kai said. "If we all live in the same house, I'd like to live in yours," he admitted.

"Oh?" Lake asked.

"Yeah, your house is a lot bigger and I like my room at your place better. Plus, I don't have to share a bathroom at your house," Kai said. Lake chuckled and messed his son's hair.

"Bathroom time is very important to a guy, right?" Lake asked. Kai smiled and nodded.

"Mom hogs the bathroom fixing her hair and make-up. She says that she needs all the help she can get in there," Kai said, making a face.

Lake laughed, "Well, I won't tell your mom you said that if you tell her that it was your idea that we bring dinner to her." Lake didn't want Star getting her hopes up and showing up with dinner for her would give her that—hope. The last time they had dinner together, they ended up naked in the back of his pick-up and Lake was pretty sure that would be an awful idea.

"Deal," Kai agreed. "Can you throw in some ice cream?" he asked. His kid was a bottomless pit.

"You drive a hard bargain," Lake teased. "But, I think I can handle that."

THEY GOT BACK to the reservation by dinner time and Kai seemed excited about the three of them sharing a meal. On the drive back, he went on and on about them picking Star's favorite pasta dish for dinner, and how surprised she was going to be. Lake wasn't as excited about their dinner but when Kai settled in for the night, he and Star were going to have to sit down and get a few things straight. They were also going to have to decide when and how they were going to tell Kai that they weren't getting married. Sooner or later, they would need to end the charade and now that it was affecting Kai, it was going to have to be sooner.

Lake pulled into her gravel driveway and noted the pick-up truck sitting next to her own. "You know who's truck that is?" he asked Kai.

"Nope," Kai said. Lake worried that Dane was paying Star an unwelcome visit. He had called her several times and even showed up at her school a few times until her lawyer got involved and got her and Kai a restraining order. There was no way that he wanted Kai walking into a shitstorm if Dane had managed to get into Star's cabin.

"Wait in the truck," Lake ordered. "Lock yourself in and don't open the door for anyone but me or your mother—got it?"

"Yes," Kai said. Lake hated the fear he saw in his son's eyes.

"Everything will be fine, Kai," he promised and shut his door. Lake walked to the front porch and didn't bother with knocking. He wanted to use the element of surprise if that was even possible. He stepped into the small entryway and found Star sitting in the family room with Kyle Burros. If he wasn't mistaken, Kyle was the math teacher for the high school and worked in the same building as Star.

She stood and crossed the room, meeting Lake at the front door. "What are you doing here?" she asked. "Where's Kai? I thought you were keeping him all night at your place." He looked past her to where Kyle sat back on her sofa and smiled.

"You planned on having a sleepover?" Lake asked.

"What—no," Star insisted. Poor Kyle's smile quickly faded. Guess she forgot to tell Kyle that he wasn't spending the night.

"What the hell are you thinking, Star?" he growled. "We're engaged."

"Really, Lake?" she questioned. Star put her hands on her hips and shook her head at him as if challenging him to come out with the truth.

"You want to do this now?" he asked. "What about your company?"

She turned back to Kyle and smiled, "I'm sorry, Kyle. I think my plans for the night have changed and my son is home. Raincheck on dinner?" she asked.

"Sure thing, Star," Kyle said, standing to gather his things. "We'll celebrate another night." He strode past where she and Lake stood and nodded to her. "Night, Star," he breathed.

Star waved and when the door shut, she stared down Lake, "What the hell was that Lake?" she asked.

"Well, I not an expert but I think that looked like a date," he said.

"Not what I was doing—you barging into my home and running my friend off," she said.

"Friend?" Lake questioned. "He looked to be more than a friend, Stardust." He only used her whole name when he was upset with her and right now, he was downright pissed. How could she blow their story like this? He had worked so hard to make everyone in town believe that he and Star were a couple and now, the whole town would be talking about Star being on a date with the math teacher.

"So what if he is more than just a friend, Lake?" she asked. "You've made it clear that you're not interested in me. Why shouldn't I find someone to be with if you don't want me?" He wanted her, that wasn't the problem. The issue he had was that his head was having a hard time forgetting what his heart so easily had.

"Because the town and our son believes that we're getting married. How do you think Kai would have felt walking in here interrupting your date?" Lake asked.

Star sighed, "It wasn't a date," she breathed. "Kyle's up for teacher of the year and I asked him over to have dinner—to celebrate. It wasn't anything else. Kyle and I are friends from high school and I'm pretty sure that no one will think that Kyle and I are dating behind your back," she said.

"Why's that?" Lake questioned.

Star smiled up at him, "Because he's gay," she said. God, he was an idiot. "Um, where's Kai?" she asked.

"Shit," Lake cursed. "In the truck. He misses you and wanted to bring you dinner home. He's asking questions about us getting married and I'm not sure how to answer them."

"Oh God," Star said. "Like what kind of questions?"

"Well, for one, he wants to know where we're going to live once we're married. He's also questioning why you never do anything with us," Lake said.

"Crap," Star said. "You tell him anything yet?"

"No—I wasn't sure what to tell him. I thought that we should talk and come up with a plan—you know like a united front?" he asked.

"Sure," she said.

"I think we're going to have to tell him," Lake said.

"It's too soon," she countered. "If we tell Kai that we lied to him again, he'll take off, or worse. I think we should stick to the plan and stage a break-up. It'll be just as much for him as it will be for the rest of the town."

"Mom," Kai said, peeking his head in through the front door. "Is it safe? I have to pee."

"Sorry bud," Lake said. "Everything's fine."

"Who was that man?" Kai asked.

"Just a friend from work," Star said. "Kyle is a math teacher at the school and he's up for an award."

"Okay," Kai said. "Can I use the bathroom?" he asked.

"Yes, you may," Star said. Kai ran past her back to the cabin's only bathroom and Lake chuckled.

"I'll run out to my truck and grab dinner. You eat yet?" he asked. Star shook her head. He could tell that she was still upset with him for barging in on her and Kyle but he didn't care. They needed to come up with a plan because he wouldn't be able to keep up this charade for much longer.

STARDUST

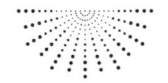

Spending the night with Lake and Kai wasn't the plan but it turned out to be a good night. They didn't spend much time together—the three of them. It was Lake's plan—telling her that he wanted some one-on-one time with Kai, to get to know him, but she knew the truth. He was using every excuse in the book to avoid her and that hurt.

Kai had asked Lake to tuck him in and she used her free time to clean the kitchen. She also shot Kyle a quick text telling him again how sorry she was that their plans got messed up. He told her that it wasn't a big deal but as one of her only friends in town, it was a big deal to her. Kyle had a rough time growing up being different from everyone else. When he came out, he was all but shunned but Star stood beside him and he always returned the favor. Kyle was one of the first teachers to welcome her back to town when she got the job as the school's librarian. And, when everyone in town was talking about her sudden engagement to Lake, Kyle was one of the first to congratulate her. Through it all, she never told Kyle or anyone else, for that matter, that she and Lake were just pretending and it sure would be nice to have someone to talk to about everything now. Lake told his sisters about the rouse but talking to either of them wasn't an option. It felt wrong to spill her guts to Lake's family.

His father was still MIA and she knew that Lake was having a hard time with that. He had taken off the day Lake's mother passed and he hadn't heard from his dad since. Kaiah and Aylen were trying to track him down but Echo didn't seem to want to be found. Star knew that Lake missed his dad, but he was so angry at him and at her, he was finding it hard to forgive any of them.

"He's out," Lake whispered.

"Thanks," she said. "I'm sorry that he didn't end up at your place tonight. I know you value your time with Kai," she said.

"Well, he seemed to be missing you and I'd never keep him from you. He needs both of us, Star," Lake whispered. He sat down next to her on the sofa; his leg so close to hers that they were almost touching.

"I'm not the one keeping the three of us apart, Lake. You said that you needed time just the two of you, so you could get to know Kai. I'm giving that to you," she said. Every time Lake picked up Kai, leaving her behind felt like she was being abandoned. It was silly really, but she was so lonely without Kai that she often spent the evenings crying and watching old movies to pass the time. "I miss him so much when he's with you," she whispered.

"You seem to be getting along fine tonight," he accused.

Star rolled her eyes and even laughed. He was still hung up on Kyle being at her place tonight. "I told you that he's a friend from high school. We work together and he's gay Lake. You know what that means, right?" she teased. "I'm not his type," she said.

"I know what gay means, Stardust. I'm just saying that you seem to be filling your time without Kai and me around," he said.

Star barked out her laugh, "You know that most nights when you have Kai, I sit right here and cry while watching an old, sappy movie. I'm miserable without him. Hell, Lake, I'm miserable without both of you but you're the most stubborn person I've ever met."

"You lied to me and kept me from my son," Lake reminded.

"And, I'm paying the price," she spat. "How much longer are you going to punish me, Lake?" she questioned.

"That's not what I'm doing, Star," he whispered. "I'm getting to know Kai. We both needed some time."

"Okay—I've given you some time. What's next, Lake?" she asked. "When do we get to the next step in all of this?"

"Next step?" Lake asked.

"Yeah," she said, "you know the part I'm talking about—where you break up with me and this fake engagement. The part where we tell the town that we've changed our minds and have decided to go our separate ways."

"It's not time for that yet," he said.

"According to what? Do you have a calendar that you're keeping track of all this on?" she questioned.

"Of course I don't," he said. "That would be ridiculous."

"This whole thing is ridiculous," she almost shouted. Star looked back down the hallway to make sure that Kai wasn't awake from her shouting—that would be the last thing they needed. "I just can't do this anymore, Lake. I won't pretend that I'm happily engaged to you anymore. I'd rather tell everyone the truth and let the pieces fall where they may."

"We did this to protect Kai," Lake reminded. "I did it to protect you." That was the first time he had admitted that fact, even though it was something Star hoped was true.

"I don't need protection, Lake," she breathed. "I appreciate what you did for me, but I feel like I've been living a lie. I've done enough of that to last me a lifetime," she said. "For the past ten years, I've been lying to everyone around me, including my son, and ultimately, you. Coming back here was something I did, not only for you and Kai to get to know each other, but to give up the charade that was my life. When I left Dane, I promised myself that I wasn't going to be that person anymore. Telling you the truth was my first step, but I have so much more to do. Maybe it's time I was truthful with the rest of the town."

"You aren't lying to the town, I am," he defended.

"I am too, by pretending to be engaged to you. How do you think Kai's going to feel when he finds out that we aren't getting married? What happens if he finds out that we never really were engaged?" she asked.

"He doesn't have to find out," Lake said.

"Kai already suspects that something's up. Everyone's starting to talk about the fact that you and I aren't ever in the same room together. We don't act like two people in love who can't wait to spend the rest of our lives together. They're putting two and two together and I'm betting that people are smart enough to figure it out."

Lake stood and walked across the room to her front door, "Just think this through," he said. "I won't force you into something you don't want to do. But, I won't hurt Kai. Telling everyone the truth and letting them gossip about you, isn't an option for me either." Lake pulled her front door open and walked out into the night leaving her confused and for the first time in a long time, hopeful.

STAR WOKE in the middle of the night to Kai standing over her bed. "Mom," he whispered, "I think someone is at the front door." Star sat up in her bed, waking up quickly. "I heard a banging," Kai whispered.

"Okay baby," she said, "I want you to stay here in my bed and call your dad on my cell," she said, handing her phone to him. Kai climbed up into her bed and nodded. "Good. Tell your dad to come over right away and you stay right here for me, got it?" she asked, tucking the blankets around him. He nodded again.

"Be careful, Mom," he ordered as she pulled on her shoes.

"Will do, Honey," she said. "I'll be fine," she promised. "I'm a badass wolf, remember?" she smiled back at her son and almost wanted to laugh when he frowned back at her. "Stay," she said, pointing at him. Kai watched her leave and she could almost feel his fear. She hoped that he was wrong and that no one was at her little cabin but she knew better. Her wolf was on high alert and she could almost smell him—Dane. He had come back but why? Why now, after all this time?

The last time she saw her ex, he was standing on her doorstep, telling Lake that he was Kai's dad, and promising her that he'd never give her or Kai a penny. That was just fine with her—she didn't want his damn money, but why come back? Dane's lawyer sent the signed divorce papers to her lawyer just a few days prior, and she thought that would be the last she'd hear from him. She asked for nothing except for him to sign off on Kai's last name change and parental rights, which he had done.

Star peaked out the front window to find Dane staring back in at her and from the looks of him, he was drunk. "It's three in the morning, Dane," she shouted through the window pane.

"Open the fucking door," he shouted back at her. "We need to talk." Star wanted to tell him that they had nothing to talk about. That time for talking was long past due but she also knew that her ex wouldn't leave until he got what he wanted. She knew that Dane would continue to bang on her front door until she talked to him.

She sighed and went to the front door, pulling it open. She slipped past him and onto the front porch, not wanting to invite him into her home—not with Kai just inside. "You wanted to talk?" she questioned, "Then, talk," she ordered, knowing how much her ex-husband hated being ordered around.

"You're engaged?" he asked. Wow—news had traveled fast and far.

"How did you find out?" she asked.

"Media," he said. Dane was pacing her porch and he looked so lost that she almost felt bad for him. "I was doing a fucking news conference and the reporter asked me how I felt about my ex-wife being engaged just days after I signed the divorce papers. Hell, Star," he growled, "the ink on our paperwork isn't even dry yet and you're agreeing to marry another guy? How do you think that makes me look? How do you think it looks to my fans who adore me?" She barked out her laugh at his mention of being adored. It was what Dane loved about being somewhat famous—that people adored him. Honestly, it was mostly women who adored him and if they only knew what an abusive asshole Dane was, they'd quickly change their minds about him.

"I see that you've stayed in touch with your modest side, Dane," she sassed.

"This isn't funny, Star," he shouted. "This is important and you're fucking it all up. I should have been given a heads up that you're rushing into another marriage."

"I'm not rushing into anything and who I'm with and what I'm doing isn't any of your business anymore," she spat. She knew she was poking the bear but like she told her son, she was a badass wolf who could take care of herself. The problem with that would be exposing herself as a shifter. Not only that, but she'd expose her son and possibly her pack and tribe, and Star couldn't do that to any of them. If her wolf showed up to the fight with Dane, she'd tear her ex apart and that would end badly for her.

Dane towered over her as if almost daring her to say those words to his face. "It became my business when my after game press conference turned into twenty questions about you," he insisted. Dane hated when the attention wasn't on him and having a reporter ask about her had to be a giant blow to his ego. He liked to be in the spotlight.

"Listen, Dane," she said. "I don't want any trouble. Kai is sleeping and it's a school night. Please, just leave, and let's forget any of this ever happened." She didn't want to threaten him, telling him that she'd call the police. That would only provoke her ex, and that was the last thing she wanted.

"You're with him, aren't you?" he asked. "You're engaged to Kai's biological father, right?" She knew that giving Dane the truth would only piss him off further and that wasn't something she was willing to do—not with Kai just inside the house. She just hoped her son called Lake, like she ordered because she could use some back up right about now.

"It doesn't matter, Dane. None of this matters. You need to go home and sleep it off. Are you staying at a local hotel? I can give you a ride—you shouldn't be driving." How he had gotten out to her cabin without killing himself or someone else was beyond her. She could smell the alcohol on his breath and knew that he was too intoxicated to legally drive.

"I don't need your help or your pity," he spat. "I shouldn't have ever signed those damn papers. I shouldn't have given up my rights to my son. You forced me," he said, pointing an accusing finger in her direction.

"He's not your son, Dane. We've already been over this," she whispered, trying to keep her voice down so Kai wouldn't hear her.

"You never proved it," he spat. "I should have demanded proof. You just took him from me."

"I can get you your proof if that's what you need. Are you looking for closure, Dane?" she asked. He shrugged and took a step closer to her, teetering from the effects of the alcohol.

"I'm looking for revenge," he growled. "I'm looking for you to pay for all your lies, bitch," he spat. Dane grabbed her arm and spun her around, pushing her front up against the side of the cabin. She could feel the anger pouring from his big body and the last thing she wanted or needed was a confrontation.

"Don't do this, Dane," she begged. "I don't want to hurt you."

He barked out his laugh and tugged her arm back behind her body with such force that she could hear the snap of her shoulder dislocating from its socket. Star cried out in pain and Dane pressed his body up against hers, pinning her to the side of the house. Star sobbed at the pain that shot down her body from her dislocated shoulder. He was breathing against her neck and the smell of the alcohol on his breath and the horrible pain she was in made her want to hurl.

"I think it's time to remind you of what you lost," he whispered into her ear. Star heard the zipper to his jeans lower and she wanted to shout for help—scream for someone to help her. But, if Dane was going to do what she thought he was, the last thing she wanted was for her son to come to her rescue.

"Kai," she whispered her son's name as if willing him to stay in the cabin and stay safe.

Star closed her eyes, wishing that this was just a horrible

nightmare she'd wake up from, as Dane started to lower her pajama pants. "You do anything to piss me off and I'll go in there and fucking kill him, you understand. You keep your fucking mouth shut," Dane ordered. She knew he'd do it too. He'd hurt Kai or worse and she would do anything to keep her son safe—including let Dane touch her again.

A growl sounded behind them and Dane released her to spin around to see where it came from. "What the fuck?" he shouted. Star held her shoulder with her good hand and turned to find Lake's wolf standing on the porch next to Dane, staring him down.

"I think it would be best for you to leave, Dane. Lake doesn't look very happy to see you," she whispered. Star felt like she was holding her breath waiting to see what would happen next. She knew that if Dane challenged Lake, he'd end up on the ground or worse and Lake's wolf looked about ready to tear Dane to shreds if given the chance.

"This isn't fair," Dane slurred. "Fight me, man to man—make it a fair fight at least," he said. Lake's wolf snarled and took another menacing step toward Lake.

"I think he's telling you to leave, Dane. I'm not sure you understand what wolves are capable of, but I'm betting Lake's wolf would like to give you a little demonstration." Dane sneered back at her and shook his head.

"You're not going to win, Star. I won't quit until I have what I want," Dane said. He stepped past Lake's wolf and got into the rental car, giving her a mock salute as he drove off into the night.

Lake's wolf snarled as he stood beside her, watching Dane drive down the gravel path. "Yeah," she grumbled. "I feel the same way." Star winced in pain as she tried to right her clothing. She didn't want to chance Kai finding her half-naked on the porch when he realized Dane was gone. Her curious son was sure to poke his head out the front door to make sure it was all clear.

Lake shifted back to his human form and she grabbed the old quilt she kept on her porch, for when she came home from a run and handed it to him. He wrapped it around his naked body but not before she took her chance to look him over. It had been a while since she had seen Lake naked and God, he was beautiful. His sleeves of tribal tattoos that ran up both arms detailed his toned muscles that made her mouth water.

"Thanks for coming over," she whispered when she realized that he had caught her looking him over.

"Where's Kai?" he asked. Of course, his son was the reason he was there and that hurt a little.

"He's in the cabin," she said. "Thank God he didn't follow me out here because Dane was going to—" she let her words trail off, not wanting to admit out loud that Dane was going to rape her if Lake hadn't come along when he did.

"I know," Lake said. "I'm so sorry, Star."

She shrugged, "Not your fault. I just appreciate you showing up when you did."

"Did he hurt you?" Lake asked, looking at her shoulder.

"Yeah," she admitted. "I think he dislocated my shoulder." She tried to play it off like it didn't hurt like a mother fucker, but it did. "I think I need to see a doctor."

"I can pop it back into place for you and then in the morning, I can get you in to see the doc," Lake offered.

"Thanks," she said. She turned to go into the cabin and found Kai sitting on the sofa, waiting for her. She hated how worried her son looked and she crossed the room to sit next to him. "You did good, Son," she said. "Thank you for calling your dad."

"I was worried," Kai whispered. "Did dad—I mean, Dane hurt you?"

"Not too much," she lied. "Lake thinks he can fix my shoulder and I'll run into see the doctor in the morning. How about you get back to bed and try to get a few more hours sleep before we have to wake up for the day?" she asked.

He looked up at Lake, "Will you tuck me?" he asked. Lake smiled down at his son and nodded.

"Of course, buddy," he agreed. He looked back at Star, "Be right back to fix that shoulder," he said. She nodded and leaned back into the sofa, wincing at the pain it caused her. What a fucking disaster her life had turned out to be. One thing she knew for sure—Dane wasn't going to give up. He'd be back and next time, he'd be ready to face down Lake and his wolf.

LAKE

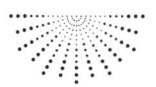

Lake found Stardust laying back on her sofa and God, she was so beautiful. Getting the phone call from Kai tonight made him realize that all the shit that they were going through, wasn't what mattered. Hearing the panic in his little boy's voice when he begged Lake to come over and help his mother—that's what mattered. Finding Dane hovering over Star, pressing her up against the side of her cabin, threatening to kill Kai and rape her—that mattered. When he saw the fear in Star's eyes and the way she bravely faced down her ex, doing exactly what he ordered to save her son—that mattered. Lake was done with all the fighting and hurt they were causing each other. He was done with his brain not listening to what his heart wanted. He was done with not trusting the one woman he'd ever loved. He was just done.

"This is going to hurt," he said. He sat down next to Star on the sofa and examined her shoulder—sure enough, it was dislocated and he'd need to pop it back into place before she started healing.

"That's okay," she whispered. "I can take it."

"Once I pop it back into place, it should start to feel better," Lake promised. She nodded and he stood beside her. "On the count of three," he said.

"Just give me a one count," she countered.

He nodded and breathed the word, "One," popping her shoulder back into the socket in one swift move. She cried out in pain, covering her mouth with her good hand as if stifling the sound. "There," he said. "You'll be as good as new in no time. You should still let me take you to the doctor in the morning."

"No need," she said, holding her arm to her side with her good hand. "I can manage. Thanks so much for stopping by," she said, making her way to the front door.

"Are you kicking me out, Star?" he teased.

"No," she said. "I know we probably woke you and you'll want to get home and back to bed. Plus, I need to figure out what to do about Dane," she whispered.

"What did he mean when he said he wouldn't quit until he has what he wants? What does that asshole want, Star?" Lake asked.

"Revenge," she murmured. She strode past him and sat back down on the sofa, wincing when her sore shoulder made contact with the back of the couch.

"What do you mean, revenge? I thought that your divorce was finalized last week?" he asked. Lake had paid attention to every detail involving her divorce, especially the parts that dissolved Dane's parental rights to Kai.

"It was finalized. He signed the papers but then he was at an after game news conference and a reporter asked him about me and you," she said.

"You and me?" he questioned.

"Yeah—he found out that we're engaged and I guess it just pissed him off. Dane told me that he wanted proof that Kai's not his son," she sobbed and he couldn't stand it anymore. Lake crossed the small family room and sat down next to her on the sofa, pulling her up against his body. She cried against his bare chest and he had to admit—it felt damn good to be holding Star in his arms again.

"Baby, all we have to do is submit to some DNA testing and that will shut him right up," Lake offered. It's what his lawyer wanted when he called to tell him about Kai. He told Lake to get a DNA test but he held off, not wanting to upset his son any more than they already had. He thought he'd have time before subjecting Kai to a DNA test.

"I know," she sniffled. "But, I hate putting you and Kai through anything else because of the choices I made. If I had only been honest from the start and listed you as Kai's biological father on his birth certificate, none of this would be happening right now." Lake kissed the top of her head and snuggled her close.

"How about a new agreement?" he asked. Star sat up and looked at him as if he'd lost his mind.

"A new agreement?" she questioned.

"Yeah—I think it's about time that we start fresh. You know, forget the shitty things that happened in the past and move forward?" Lake took Star's hand into his own and pulled her onto his lap.

"You can't be serious, Lake," she insisted. "I lied to you. I have kept you from your son for ten years. That can't be forgiven." Lake smoothed his hand down her back and pulled her in for a quick kiss.

"Already done," he promised.

"Just like that?" she asked. He could tell Star didn't trust that he had forgiven her but he had.

"Just like that," he agreed. "Seeing you tonight—what you were going to go through to keep Kai safe, I don't know why it happened or what caused it, but something inside of me just clicked and I forgave you."

"Lake—" he could tell she was going to give him a fight but he wouldn't allow it.

"Why didn't you shift tonight, Star?" he asked, interrupting her.

She shrugged, "I guess I didn't want to expose our pack. I wouldn't put it past Dane to have a camera crew waiting outside of my house to catch me or Kai shifting. He'd use the footage to blackmail me—he threatened to do that when we were together. He tried to keep both Kai and me from shifting—that way he kept the upper hand. Fear is a powerful thing," she whispered.

"And, Dane liked to keep you afraid?" he asked, but he already knew the answer.

"Yeah," she said. "It wasn't just the physical abuse; it was the emotional abuse too. I was always afraid that he'd find a way to expose who and what I was. That would ultimately expose Kai and where would we be then?" Lake wanted to tell her that they'd be right where they belonged back on the reservation with him and their pack, but he didn't know that for sure. Maybe Star needed to go through everything that Dane put her and Kai through to get to the place where she wanted to come back to him. If she returned to the reservation out of sheer need, he might never find a way to keep her. But, Star wanted to be back home and that counted for something. That fact alone gave him hope that he'd be able to keep her there with him this time and maybe she wouldn't run again.

"Dane liked to tell me that he'd hurt Kai if I shifted. He told me that he'd get proof that I was a freak, and that no judge would ever let me near my son again. I stopped shifting after a while, too afraid that he was right and that he'd find a way to take Kai away from me. But then, Kai shifted for the first time and Dane started to change his tune," she said.

"How so?" Lake asked.

"Well, it was almost like he took an interest in all things shifter because he wanted to get closer to Kai. Hell, for a while, he even thought that he might be a shifter too. He Googled wolf shifters and read that only whole blooded wolf shifters could produce shifters. He was too stupid and caught up in himself to realize that Kai wasn't his kid. Instead, he came up with the ridiculous notion that he had to be shifter too if Kai was."

"But, that's not true. Both parents don't have to be full-blooded wolves to create a pup," he protested. He thought about his sisters, Aylen and Kaiah. Aylen was a shifter and Kaiah wasn't. His father, a wolf shifter, had married their mother, a seer.

"I tried to tell Dane that but he didn't want to hear it.

With the way he went on about having shifter blood and possibly being one of us, well—it felt like he had accepted me for the first time. He accepted both Kai and me and I wasn't about to look a gift horse in the mouth. I took it as a win and let him believe what he wanted. He allowed me to shift with Kai and stopped threatening to take him away from me. But, that didn't last long."

"Things turned bad again?" he asked.

She nodded, "He started beating me again when he realized that he wasn't able to shift. He told me that I wasn't helping him enough with his training, as if I'd be able to train a human to shift into a wolf," she said, barking out her laugh. "Still, the more frustrated he grew, the more he took it out on me. One day, Kai and I had just come home from a run, and when he met us at the front door, he accused me of trying to take his son from him. Dane said that I was hogging all of Kai's time and not leaving any for him. He even went as far as to say that I was trying to drive a wedge between him and Kai. He tried to hit me and Kai stepped in the way, taking the full force of Dane's fist to his jaw. That's when I had enough and left him. The next day, while Dane was at practice, I told Kai that we were taking a little trip and to pack as much as he could. I got everything into my old car and we took off for the reservation. By the time Dane got home, we were long gone."

"He didn't follow you?" Lake asked.

"He didn't know where we were going. I never told him about this place—not until my lawyer served him with the divorce papers I had drawn up. I had to put the cabin's address on the paperwork. I just never imagined he'd show up here. That was the night you took me on our date and we came back here to find him on my porch," she said.

That was the night that changed his life—the night he found out that he had a son he didn't know about. "That was the night he told me about Kai," Lake whispered.

"Yes," she said. "It was also the night that I lost you." Star looked up at him, her big green eyes so full of hurt. He wanted to take that all away from her—all the pain, hurt, and disappointment that life had thrown at her. "You can't possibly forgive me, Lake," she said. "I've caused you so much pain that I'd never ask for your forgiveness."

"You don't have to ask for it, Star," he said. He pushed her dark hair back from her face and gently kissed her lips. "I've already given it to you. I forgive you, Star." A sob escaped her parted lips and he pulled her down onto his bare chest. "So, can we start over?" he asked again. He could feel her head nodding against his skin and he looked down and smiled. "Good," he said. "If this is going to work, we're going to need to promise each other only the truth from here on out. Can you promise me that, Star?" he asked. She nodded again and smiled up at him, through her tears.

"I promise," she whispered. "You will have my complete honesty from here on out, Lake. I'll never lie to you again."

"Thank you, Baby," he said. "You have my promise of the same. If we're going to raise Kai together, he needs us to present a united front. We're a team from here on out, got it?" he asked. Star nodded and he was almost afraid to say the next part—the part she wasn't going to so easily agree to, but it was for her and Kai's good. This was possibly the most important part of his plan because if she didn't agree to it, she and their son would be left vulnerable.

"We'll need to find a way to work our shit out and not run away anymore, Star. If things don't go as planned or you think I'm pushing you for more than you're willing to give, you promise to stick around and talk it out instead of taking off again—promise?" he asked.

"Yes," she said. "I promise not to run. This place has quickly become Kai's home now too. I won't separate you guys again," she said. "Kai needs you, Lake. He needs his father."

Now, he knew he could tell her the next part of his plan without her heading back out of town with his kid in tow. "I'm glad you feel that way, Honey, because I'm moving in here with you."

Lake gave her a minute and he almost wanted to laugh at the confusion that crossed her beautiful face. He chuckled and dipped his head for another kiss. "Wait," she said. "You're moving in here—with us?" she asked. Lake nodded and smiled, kissing her again. "Lake," she chided. "Stop trying to distract me with kisses," she demanded.

He laughed, "Why is it working?" he teased.

"Yes," she said. "And, I need to think this through."

"There's nothing to think through, Baby," he said. "I want to be close to Kai."

"Oh," she said, not letting him finish.

"Hear me out, Star," he begged. "And, I want to be close to you. I'd like to see where this all goes and well, you said that you'd try."

"I did promise you that," she said.

"I'm also worried that we haven't seen or heard the last of Dane," Lake added. "I'd like to go into town tomorrow and put in a restraining order against him. I don't want him anywhere near you or Kai."

"No," she breathed. "That will only piss him off more. You saw what happened tonight after he got the signed divorce papers and was asked a simple question about me by a reporter. I'm afraid that a restraining order will just send him over the edge and there's no telling what he's capable of. My lawyer put in a restraining order when he filed my divorce papers and look how well that's worked out for me. A piece of paper telling Dane to stay away from me, won't stop him."

"You're forgetting that we're a team now, Honey. Plus, I'm pretty sure that people around these parts are familiar with shifters. If he tries to expose any of us, no one will care. And, we have an ace up our sleeves," he said.

"What's that?" she asked.

"We can just have a DNA test done to prove I'm Kai's dad and then Dane won't have a leg to stand on," Lake said. At least, he hoped that was the case. He knew how wealthy and famous Dane was. He probably had enough money to tie things up in court for a damn long time if he wanted to, but Lake was hopeful that proving that Kai was his kid, would put a stop to Dane's nonsense.

"You think that's all it will take to stop Dane?" she asked. He didn't but he wouldn't tell her that.

"Yes," he lied. "We've got this, Honey," Lake promised. "Can I move in?" He felt as though he was holding his breath waiting for her answer.

"All right," she agreed. He kissed her again and this time, when Star wrapped her good arm around his shoulder, he stood lifting her into his arms.

"Good," he said. "Considered me moved in, Baby. Let's go back to bed." Lake carried her back to her bed and laid her across the mattress, her dark hair spilling around her. It was time to remind Stardust that she belonged to him.

STARDUST

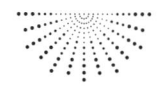

Lake hovered over her as if watching and waiting for her to give her permission for everything he wanted to do to her next. She could see it all in his hazel eyes too—every promise he silently made her, and all the dirty things he wanted to do to her body. Lake had never been shy when it came to taking her or telling her what he wanted to do to her but right now, she could tell that he was unsure of himself and Star hated that.

She reached up to cup his face with her good arm, "Yes, Lake," she whispered.

"Yes?" he asked.

"Yes, to everything you're not asking me for. I want to give you everything," she promised. "Please."

"I want to marry you, Star," he said. "I know that's what sent you running from me ten years ago but that hasn't changed for me. I still feel the same way. I want a family with you—I want more kids and this time; I want to be around for the whole thing. I want to watch my kids being born and hold your hand. Tell me that doesn't scare you off," he demanded. It should have. It had in the past but hearing everything that he wanted with her now only made her heart feel like it could beat out of her chest. She wanted all those things too and she wanted them with Lake. It should have always been with Lake but she was so foolish. She wished she could change her past but all she could do now was promise Lake her future.

"Yes," she whispered. "I want all of that with you too, Lake," she promised.

"Thank fuck," he growled. Lake dropped the quilt he had around his body and stood gloriously naked in front of her.

"I've missed you," Star admitted.

"I've missed you too, Baby," he said. "So much." She reached for him and that was all the invitation he seemed to need. Lake covered her body with is own and God, it felt like coming home being pressed up against him like she was. Lake kissed her like he missed her too, taking his time, reminding her just how well they fit. He snaked his hand down and ran his fingers through her drenched folds. "So wet for me, Star."

"Yes," she hissed. She had dreamed of Lake forgiving her and finding his way back into her life and her bed for weeks now. But, like most things, real life was so much better than her dreams. She wanted to lose herself in him and Lake seemed just as determined to make her his again.

He pulled his fingers free from her pussy and lined up his cock, thrusting into her body, taking everything that he wanted from her. "Fuck, you feel good, Honey," he whispered.

"I need you, Lake," she demanded. She was squirming and writhing under his body and he stilled. "What's wrong?" she asked.

"You keep doing that and I won't last long," he admitted. Star giggled and wrapped her arms and legs around him, holding him to her body.

"Really?" she questioned. She felt like pushing the limits with him and making him as crazy as he made her was a heady power trip. She wiggled under his big body again and he groaned, pulling almost completely out of her body and thrusting back in, causing her to moan out her pleasure.

"See, Baby," he taunted. "Turnabout is fair play, Sweetheart." He pulled out again and thrust back in through her wet folds. "I'm going to fuck you so hard; you're going to remember me, and everything we did tonight, all day tomorrow."

"I'd never be able to forget about you, Lake," she whispered. "Even after all these years, I wasn't able to forget you." Star ran her hand down his face and he leaned into her touch, closing his eyes as if savoring their connection.

"Baby," he whispered. "I never forgot you, either. I've never loved anyone else, Star," he promised. Her heart stuttered at his omission and she wasn't sure she'd be able to handle much more.

"Love me, Lake," she begged, "please."

"Always," he promised. Lake started moving, pulling her up against his body, going up on his knees between her legs.

He held her tight against his body as she straddled his lap, riding his cock.

"You feel so good," she whispered. He pumped into her body, driving her to the edge and then backing down. She could tell that he was trying to last longer but she wasn't sure that was a possibility for her. Star wanted to find her release—she needed it. "Lake," she cried out when she was close again. This time, he didn't hold back. This time, he gave her what she needed, pumping into her body like he was on a mission to drive her out of her mind. Star fell, knowing that Lake would catch her and when he came, spilling his seed deep inside of her, she lost the last little piece of her heart to him. She belonged to him now—body, mind, and soul, whether he knew it or not, she was his.

"Fuck," he swore. "That was—"

"Perfect," she finished for him. Lake rolled away from her and got out of the bed, finding his pants on the floor, and pulling them on. Her heart sank when she realized that he was getting dressed to leave. "I—I thought you were staying," she whispered. Lake looked back at her, smiling his wolfish grin that always made her heart stutter.

"I'm going to check on Kai," he said, leaning back over the bed to kiss her. "And, I want to make sure the cabin's secure. Tomorrow, I'll get Gray to come over and check things out. He owns a construction company but his business partner, Nomad, does security installation. I want this place well protected so I don't have to worry about you or Kai when I can't be here," he said. She must have looked worried when he mentioned not being able to be with them because Lake chuckled and kissed her again. "I can see your wheels turning, Honey. I won't be able to be by your side twenty-four, seven. I have to work and I'm sure there will be times when you two are here without me—it's just a precaution, Baby," he said.

"All right," she said. "I'd feel better with some extra security around here. Dane can come back at any time, I'm sure."

"And, when he does, I'll fucking kill him," Lake growled. Star knew he meant it too, but if he gave in to his anger, that would get them nowhere.

"I'd rather not visit you in prison," Star teased.

"He won't touch you or Kai again, Honey," Lake promised. "In the morning, I'll go pack up some of my stuff and bring it over. I'll move fully in over the weekend if that works for you," he said. Star wasn't quite sure what to say, it felt like her life was moving at top speed and she wasn't sure that she wanted it to slow down. Everything Lake was offering, even demanding, was what she wanted, and telling him no wasn't an option.

"Okay," she whispered.

He rubbed his thumb down her cheek, "This will be good, Baby," he said. "Promise." Lake was choosing his words carefully, making her promises but not giving her the words she so wanted to hear from him. Someday, he'd say those words again and mean them but for now, Star was thankful for all his promises and everything he offered her. That's what she'd hold on to for now—the words would come later.

LAKE

Lake was late for his first meeting, after running Kai to school for Star. He was happy that she was taking the day off. Her shoulder needed time to heal and she promised to go to the doctors as soon as she could get an appointment this morning. He planned on getting through his morning meetings, and then pick her up and drive her into the doctor. He wasn't going to take any chances that she'd decide she was fine and not go.

"Hey, Boss," Zoe stood from behind her desk and rounded it to meet him at his office door. "You need to know something before you go in there," she loudly whispered.

"What?" he questioned. He handed her his bag and grabbed a coffee cup from the cabinet above the pot, pouring himself a cup. "I've had a long night and I'm exhausted. How about we cut to the chase and you fill me in on what major shitstorm I'm in for, and I'll decide if I want to walk into my office."

Zoe smiled, "You had a long night, huh?" she asked. "Would it have anything to do with the mother of your son—the one you've been punishing by avoiding for the last month?"

"Shut the hell up and just tell me what's going on," he demanded.

"I'll take that as a yes and assume that you'll fill me in on all the dirty details," she said as if issuing him a challenge. Lake waved his hand in the air as if telling her to hurry things along. "For now, you need to know that your father is in your office waiting for you. He looks rough, Lake," she whispered that last part.

"Shit," he grumbled. "My meetings," he said.

"Have all been canceled for the day," Zoe promised. "They were easily moved until tomorrow but I'm not sure your dad will be able to wait as long."

"Where the hell has he been all this time?" Lake asked. "Why is he here now?"

Zoe shrugged, "Don't know," she admitted. "I didn't ask Echo any questions Lake and you shouldn't either. He looks like he just needs some understanding—maybe even someone to just listen to him. Give your dad that, Lake," she said. Lake knew his friend was right but he still had so many unanswered questions. He could put them aside—for a while, as long as his dad was safe. He just needed to see him for with his own eyes.

"Thanks, Zoe," he said. "I'll try to keep that in mind." He turned the doorknob and pushed his way into his office, finding his father sitting behind his desk in his chair.

"Dad," Lake said, nodding to his father. He stood and

crossed Lake's office to pull him into his arms, giving him one of his famous bear hugs.

"Missed you, son," Echo whispered, holding him close.

"Well, I've been here this whole time, Dad," he said. Lake stepped away from his father and rounded his desk, sitting down in his chair. "I was here for Mom's funeral and had to make all the decisions for what to do after she passed. I was here for it all, Dad. Where were you?" Echo sunk into the chair in front of Lake's desk and ran his hands over his face. For the first time since coming into the room, Lake realized just what Zoe was talking about—his old man looked rough and he felt a little guilty for being an ass, but he wanted to know.

"I couldn't take being here without your mother," Echo whispered. "Anita was my life and to watch her waste away like that was bad enough. I couldn't stick around and say goodbye to her."

"You did the hard part, Dad. You were with her until the bitter end," Lake said. His father had sat by his mother's bedside, day in and day out, reading to her and taking care of her. He wouldn't let the nurses from hospice do much of anything besides give Anita medication, to help her remain comfortable. Lake couldn't even sit and watch his mom fade to nothing like his dad had. The man was a saint, shoving his hurt down and being there for his wife, but the moment she passed away, Echo took off. At first, Lake thought that he would be back—that he just needed some time to process everything. On the morning of the funeral, after all the decisions were made, he realized that his dad wasn't coming back any time soon. Kaiah and Aylen helped Lake through everything and he was so thankful that he had them both.

"I know but that was all I had to give, Lake. I did that part for your mom because she deserved the best from me. She deserved to have everything—my love and devotion, right up to the bitter end. So, I stuck by her side and got through—for her. But once she was gone, there wasn't a reason for me to stick around."

"Gee, thanks," Lake grumbled.

"You know what I mean, Son. You're a grown man and I knew that you had your sisters to help you through. From what I've heard, you did just fine. I was told the service was beautiful and she would have loved it," Echo praised.

"That's beside the point, Dad," Lake shouted. He cleared his throat and sat back in his seat, trying to calm down. Zoe was right, his father needed a little compassion and he'd find a way to choke down his anger and give that to him. "You should have been there to say goodbye to her," Lake said.

"I did say goodbye to your mother, son. I just did it in my way and now, I'm back," Echo said. "When you love someone as much as I loved your mother, you'll understand."

"I do love someone like that, Dad. I've loved her for ten years now but you left and missed out on everything that happened," Lake accused.

"I heard that Stardust moved back to the reservation. I hear that she has a kid now too," his father said.

"Yeah—Kai's a great kid," Lake said, his smile easy. "You should come by Star's cabin sometime. I'm living out there now and I'm sure your grandson would like to meet you." He smiled at his dad, waiting him out. He could see the realization dawn on Echo's face as soon as he worked it all out.

"The kid's yours?" Echo asked.

"Yep—you have an almost ten-year-old grandson," Lake proudly boasted.

"Well, shit," his father breathed. "She didn't tell you all these years?"

"It's a long story, Dad, but Star and I are working things out—slowly. She's agreed to marry me though." Lake thought it almost comical the way his father looked at him.

"Marry you," Echo grunted. "She lied to you about having your son," he accused.

"And, I just told you that it's a long story and that we're working things out. I'm in love with her Dad and letting her go over a stupid mistake isn't something I'm willing to do," Lake explained. "You of all people now know that life's short. I decided that I can sit around and be angry at her for the rest of my life, or I can find a way to forgive her and have the life I want. It's always been Star, Dad. I want to build a life with her and I'm not willing to give up that dream. She's here now and trying to make things right and that's all that matters."

"So, I'll get to meet Kai—is that his name?" Echo asked.

"Yes," Lake said. "And, yeah—I'm sure he'd love to meet you, Dad. He hasn't grown up with much family and he loves Kaiah and her kids. Aylen and her gang are coming up in a couple of months and I'm hoping he can get to know all of his cousins, aunts, and uncles."

Echo chuckled, "You know, for being an only child for a damn long time, you sure have taken to having older sisters.

I guess if I expected you to forgive me all those years ago, for keeping your sisters from you, I should expect the same treatment for Star. You should forgive her and hell, marry her as soon as she'll agree to it. Don't waste time, son because you're right, it's precious." Lake stood and started for the door.

"You sticking around now, Dad?" Lake asked. He hoped that his father was home for good now but he wouldn't force him to stay if it was too painful being back in town.

"Yeah," Echo agreed. "I've got another grandson to get to know and I'm too tired to run off again. I'm staying."

"Good," Lake said. "How about coming out to Star's cabin for dinner in two nights? You can meet Kai and we can catch up."

"Sounds like a plan," his father agreed. "Thanks, Son," he said and walked out of his office. It was good to have his old man around again. Lake just hoped he meant it and he'd be sticking around this time. As for Star, he knew that his father was right—about everything. The sooner he got her to say, "I do," the better.

"Zoe," Lake called. She breezed into his office and smiled.

"I take it that your meeting with your dad went well?" she asked.

"Yep," Lake agreed. "Can you clear my calendar for the rest of the week?" Zoe looked at him as if he had lost his mind and hell, maybe he had. "And, can you also get Judge Roberts down here by lunchtime today?" he added.

Zoe stepped into his office and put her hands on her hips. "What are you planning, Lake Sani?" she asked.

Lake chuckled, "I'm planning on getting hitched if you'll

help me get everything thrown together in the next few hours," he said. "I'm pretty sure that my bride to be is skipping out of her doctor's appointment because she is as stubborn as the day is long. I also know that she's taking the day off to go to the doctor. So, let's just give her a proper reason to skip the doctors."

"I have no idea what any of that means but, I'm in. I love surprises," she said. "And, I love weddings," she added.

"Good," Lake said. "Arrange for the Judge to meet us here at noon and clear my schedule. I'll take care of the rest."

ZOE and he spent the rest of the day getting everything arranged. He even got his sister, Kaiah, involved and had her make up some bogus excuse to get Star down to his office, which was no easy feat. His favorite part was when his woman told Kaiah that she couldn't help her out because she had to get her shoulder checked at the doctors. Lake called the only doctor in town and they told him that Star had canceled her appointment saying that she felt, "Much better". He smiled when they said that they explained that she should have it checked, just in case, but she said that she was going to help her friend, Kaiah, with a few things and wouldn't be able to make it in. Yeah—she was playing both sides and that made him chuckle. His girl would keep him on his toes, that was for sure, but he was starting to realize that living without Star and her crazy, stubborn streak wasn't something he was willing to do.

By the time he could hear Star and his sister carrying on

in the hallway outside of his office, he had everything and everyone in place down in the courtroom. There were perks of being the tribe's chief and working at the town hall—including being able to get married at the drop of the hat with a few phone calls.

"Lake," Star called from just outside of his office.

"In here," he said. He had changed into his good suit and was holding a bouquet of white roses. She strode through his door and found him standing in the middle of his office, waiting for her. Lake had been waiting for Star for so damn long, he didn't want to wait another second for her to be his, now that she agreed to marry him.

"Marry me," he said, holding the flowers out to her.

Star giggled and rolled her eyes, "I've already said that I will marry you, Lake," she said. "You didn't need to have your sister drag me down here."

"I was kind of not being one-hundred-percent honest with you," Kaiah said, squinching up her nose.

"Wait-what?" Star asked.

"Yeah—I found out that you were planning on skipping out on your doctor appointment," Lake accused.

"So, to punish me, you decided to drag my ass down here and ask me to marry you again?" Star teased. His sister giggled and he shot her a look.

"Me asking you to marry me is a punishment?" he questioned.

"I'm just saying—I'd rather be home watching Real Housewives on my first day off in weeks," she said.

"Oh—I love them," Kaiah gushed, going completely off-topic. "Which is your favorite?"

"I love them all but I'm really into the New York Housewives right now," Star said. "Which is your favorite?" she asked. Lake groaned his frustration, drawing their attention back to himself.

"Can we focus here, Sis?" he asked. "You had a mission and you're kind of fucking things up."

"Yeah—sorry," she said, shooting him a sheepish grin. "We can talk House Wives later," she offered. "Right now, my brother wants to marry you—like today."

Lake groaned again and Star looked back at him. "Is that true?" she asked. Lake smiled and nodded, thrusting the white roses at her again.

"Only if you want to, Star. I'm done waiting for our life together to start. Marry me—now, here, today," he said. Hell, he sounded more like he was begging but he didn't care.

"What about Kai?" she asked, taking the flowers from him. "Shouldn't our son be here for this?" Lake took her hand and pulled her along beside him, down to the courtroom, pushing open the giant wooden doors to reveal Kaiah's brood, the judge who had agreed to marry them, and Kai.

"I've taken care of that," Lake said.

"He got me out of school and I had a math test," Kai boasted, causing Kaiah to giggle again.

"Great," Star grumbled.

"Don't worry," Lake said. "I've explained everything to his teacher and he can take the test tomorrow."

"I'll make sure he studies tonight," Kaiah promised.

"Why will you be helping him study for his math test?" Star asked, looking at Kaiah as if she had lost her mind.

"Because he's going to be staying with me while you and Lake are on your honeymoon," Kaiah said. "You are a lug head," she grumbled at Lake. "You could have at least given her a head's up."

Zoe walked into the back of the courtroom, holding the only thing stopping up their nuptials—the marriage certificate. "You were right in your assessment, Kaiah. Lake's a lug head and he doesn't get that some women want flowers and romance—you know a big wedding with all the bells and whistles. I hope you're okay with all this, Star. If not, blame Lake," Zoe teased handing Lake the certificate.

Star looked at him and smiled, "It's perfect," she whispered. "Thank you."

"Is that a yes?" Lake asked. "You'll marry me here and now?" Star looked around the room her eyes resting on Kai as if asking their son what she should do.

Kai nodded, "Marry him, Mom," he said. "I think that you and my dad should be together." That was the first time that Kai had called Lake his "Dad" out loud and God, it made his heart stutter. Star smiled and nodded, "Looks like we're having a wedding," she agreed. "Will you be my matron of honor?" Star asked Kaiah. His sister squealed and jumped up and down like a schoolgirl.

"Yes," she agreed. "I'm going to have a new sister," she told the entire courtroom.

"And, Kai," Lake said, clearing his throat, "will you be my best man?" he asked. Kai smiled at him and nodded.

"Great," Judge Roberts said. "Let's get this wedding started." Lake chuckled knowing that the judge wanted to get back to the golf game he had been summonsed from. It was

Judge Robert's day off but Lake didn't feel bad for interrupting his game. He'd do just about anything to make Star his—officially.

THE CEREMONY WAS quick and that was just fine by him. As long as Star was legally his wife, that was all he cared about. Well, that and their honeymoon. Lake hadn't told her about his plans yet, but he was hoping she'd agree. He wanted to spend the week with her—no distractions, no work, and no ex showing up to her cabin crazy and drunk. He had arranged for Kai to stay out at Gray and Kaiah's place and he seemed pretty happy about spending time with his cousins. Hell, Kai had even told Lake that he hoped he'd get a little brother or sister soon and Lake had to admit—he wouldn't mind that. He'd just have to get Star on board the baby train.

"You surprised me," Star whispered. He had told her that she needed to pack a bag—warm clothing and be ready to leave in thirty minutes. She didn't give him any fight and when they dropped Kai off at Kaiah's she seemed excited about getting out of town.

"Is that a good thing?" he asked. He knew that Star wasn't a big fan of surprises, at least she hadn't been when they were first together. Lake realized that there was so much he didn't know about Star. A lot had happened in ten years and he knew that they weren't the same people they used to be. They had Kai now and he was sure there would be other things he needed to learn about his new wife.

"Yeah," she said, smirking over at him. "But, you know I'm not a fan of surprises."

"I remember," he said.

"So, how about you tell me where we're headed then? You know, take some of the surprise out of it?" she said.

"Where would the fun in that be?" Lake teased

"For one, I'd know that I packed the right clothing for our trip. Second, I'd be able to start panicking now, if you plan on us flying someplace," she said. He reached for her hand and she quickly took it.

"I also remember how much you hate flying, so, we are driving. You brought your passport, right?" he asked.

"Yes," she said.

"Good," he said. "You still love skiing, right?" he asked. She smiled and nodded her head. "Well, then, I think you'll be happy with our honeymoon destination."

Star's smile quickly faded, "What happens if Dane comes looking for us? What happens if he finds out that we got married and left Kai with your sister?" she asked.

"First, Gray and my father are well aware of what's going on with your ex. They won't let him get anywhere near Kai. Second, if he comes back, the authorities will be called in and this time, we won't let him just drive off. This time, you'll be pressing charges," Lake growled.

"Okay," she whispered. "I wanted to do that so many times—press charges. But, he always said he was sorry and that it would never happen again. I was such a fool." Lake squeezed her hand into his own.

"That's all over now, Baby. Remember, we said we'd wipe

the slate clean? The past is in the past and we can't change it so, why worry about it?" he asked.

"I promise I will try not to worry if you promise that we can call home to check on Kai a few times. This will be the first extended period that we're apart," she said.

"Deal," he agreed. He hated being away from Kai too. In such a short amount of time, his son and Star had come to mean everything to him. He was going to miss reading Kai stories before tucking him into bed. It had become part of their routine.

"So, we're going skiing?" she asked, picking up on his not so subtle hint asking if she still liked skiing.

"Yep—in Bozeman, Montana. I rented us a little cabin out there and we're going to do some skiing," he said. "Or, we could just stay in bed the whole week—your call." She giggled at Lake and shook her head.

"Nope," she said. "I'd like to get in a little skiing too. It's been ages since I've been skiing thank you for coming up with this trip."

"Anytime, Honey," he promised. "I know things have been rocky between us, but I meant it when I said I'd like a clean slate. You're mine now and so is Kai—that's all that matters. From here on out, we're a team."

Star nodded, "Agreed."

"So, a week full of skiing it is," he said.

"Well, how about a week full of staying in bed with a few ski breaks," she challenged. Lake chuckled and pulled her hand up to his mouth, gently kissing her knuckles.

"Now, that's a good deal, Honey," he teased.

STARDUST

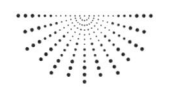

They had spent half a week blissfully snuggled into their little rental cabin, and it was perfect. She wasn't sure why Lake had made her pack so many clothes since he wasn't giving her much of a chance to wear them. He kept her naked and in bed most of the time. They had managed to go out skiing twice and he promised to take her shopping in town later this week, before heading home. She wanted to get a few souvenirs to remember their trip and something for Kai.

Star was missing her son but she was grateful to have alone time with Lake. They needed it after everything they had been through. Just before Kai's bedtime every night, Lake would call back home and read him a story and tuck him in virtually. It was the sweetest thing Star had ever seen and she was so happy that Kai and Lake finally had the relationship she always dreamed of for them. Tonight, she was sitting by the fire in the great room, waiting for Lake to finish reading to Kai. She was completely naked and sprawled out on the fake bear skin rug, just as Lake ordered. He was bossy as hell and she had to admit—she liked it. She didn't remember Lake being so bossy when they were younger but taking orders from him now was a complete turn on.

"Shit," she heard him shout from the upstairs bedroom. "You called the police, right?" he asked. He ran down the stairs to find her, helping her up from the floor.

"What happened?" she asked. Lake held up a finger, telling her to wait. Every hair on her body was standing on end and she knew it wasn't something she was going to want to hear.

"Will do," Lake said. "Keep us in the loop." He ended his call and tossed his cell onto the sofa.

"What's going on?" she asked again. Lake pulled her against his body and kissed her forehead. "You're scaring me, Lake," she said when he made no move to answer her.

"Dane showed up on the reservation. He asked around and found out about our ceremony and where Kai was staying. He was stupid enough to go out to Gray and Kaiah's and they called the police," Lake breathed.

"Do they have him? Did they take him into custody?" she asked.

"Yep," Lake said. He smiled and pulled her down to the sofa so she was laying on top of him. "They got him and he won't be able to get near you or Kai again."

Star wanted to believe the news but she had gone through enough with Dane to know that her ex was crafty and wouldn't stay behind bars for long. Lake ran his hands over her ass and smiled. "I think we should celebrate," he said, swatting her ass. "Let's go out to dinner tonight."

"What happens if he makes bail?" she questioned, not answering his offer of dinner.

Lake sighed, "Kai is safe," he promised. "Gray won't let anything happen to our son, Baby."

"You don't know what Dane is capable of," she cried. The last thing Star wanted to do was ruin their night together. She wanted to put on a pretty dress and do her hair and make-up for him. She wanted to tell him that she'd love to go to dinner with him, but the only thing she wanted to do was run back home to be with Kai. He had been her responsibility for so long she wasn't sure how to let anyone else do that job for her. She trusted Gray and Kaiah with Kai but she also knew that her ex had a way of getting what he wanted and didn't care who he hurt to do it. Kai would be a casualty in Dane's pursuit to get to her, and he'd be fine with that.

"I'm so sorry Lake but I—" He covered her mouth with his hand, not letting her finish.

"You need to go home," he whispered.

"Yes," she said. "I'm sorry but I know Dane and he won't let being arrested stop him from what he wants. He told me that he wants revenge and he'll stop at nothing to get it. He thinks that I've ruined his life and he's partially correct. I lied to him about Kai being his son and now, he wants me to pay for that lie. He'll make bail and he'll come after our son, Lake," she sobbed. Lake held her so closely that she could feel his heart beating. "He wants to hurt me and he'll use Kai to do it."

"Then, we'll go home," Lake agreed. "Pack up your things and we'll head home tonight."

"You'll have to drive all night," she said.

"I don't mind. Besides, you're right—you know Dane better than anyone. If you have a bad feeling about things then we'll head back home and get Kai. Heck, you can pick him up from school tomorrow, if you want." Star went up on her tiptoes and kissed him.

"Thank you," she whispered. "I don't deserve you."

Lake shrugged and laughed, "Probably not, but you're stuck with me, Honey," he said. "Now, go pack, woman," he said, swatting her ass as she ran upstairs to get their stuff together.

She turned back to face him, "What about the rest of our honeymoon?" She asked.

Lake smiled at her, "We can just continue it at home. Besides, the more time I spend here, the more I think we should come back soon and bring Kai next time. He'd love the snowboarding trails."

"He would," Star agreed. "I love that idea, Lake. Thank you," she turned and ran the rest of the way up the stairs to the master. She couldn't wait to get back home. Time alone with Lake was wonderful but she missed Kai.

STAR SLEPT part of the way home and felt a little guilty that Lake was doing all the heavy lifting. He needed some rest and when they were about three hours from home, she offered to drive and he jumped at the chance to get some shut-eye. She didn't mind. She was an early bird and although she didn't usually get up at three in the morning, it wasn't too bad.

She had to pull off for gas since they were just about empty, and when she got back in the car from pumping, Lake's phone chimed, letting him know that he had a message. She worried that it was Gray or Kaiah and that something happened to Kai, so she checked to see what the message was, counting herself lucky that he didn't lock his phone. It was an email from Doc. He was the only doctor on the reservation and she thought about not opening it, but then she saw Kai's name in the subject heading and she started to worry. She opened the message and read it.

"What the hell?" she asked.

Lake stirred and stretched next to her and found her holding his cell phone. "What's wrong?" he asked. "Is it Kai?"

"Yes, it's Kai," she spat. "You had a DNA test done on my son without my permission?" she asked.

"Well, it was supposed to be a surprise," he said. "I had Doc do a quick test the morning we got married. I pulled Kai from school for the ceremony and we talked about whether or not he wanted to have the test done. It was his decision, Star. We both wanted to know for certain—not that we didn't trust you," he said, holding his hands up as if in defense. "Kai said he wanted scientific proof that I'm his dad. He's a smart kid, you know. He said that maybe Dane would leave us all alone if he knew for sure that I'm his dad, so he asked me to take him to have it done."

"Oh," Star breathed, feeling a bit foolish at getting mad over the paternity test. "Kai wanted it?"

"We both did," Lake said. "I can't explain it. I know he's my kid. I one hundred percent believed you when you told me he's mine. But, we both agreed that it would be nice to have something in writing—you know, like proof." She did understand that. Being legally married to Lake made her feel like she belonged to him even more than just telling him that she loved him. It was like having the piece of paper that said that they were legally bound made it all the more real for her.

"I was going to surprise you once we got home. Kai wanted to tell you about the results and he even wanted to make a cake to celebrate," Lake said. He took his phone from her and read over the report. "I guess the cat's out of the bag though."

"How about we let Kai tell me, just as the two of you planned. You can even make a cake and then we can celebrate—just the three of us. Don't tell him I know. I can act surprised," she said.

Lake chuckled. She was the worst at keeping secrets and acting surprise wasn't her strong suit. He remembered throwing her a make-shift surprise birthday party when they were first together and she found out about it. She didn't tell him she knew but when she walked into the cabin and her small group of friends shouted, "Surprise," he could see it on her face that she wasn't.

"Okay, Baby. We'll work on your surprised face. But, I'm sure Kai will love your efforts," Lake said. She shut the truck door and started the engine.

"How about we just get home and then you help me practice my surprised face. You can jump out at me—naked and

I'll act very surprised."

Lake laughed, "Perfect," he agreed.

THEY ROLLED into town just as the sun was coming up and by the time they got to the reservation, it was breakfast time. She was exhausted and starving. Star wanted breakfast and then bed, in that order. They called Gray to let him know that they were back in town early and would pick up Kai from school but until then, she planned on spending the day naked and napping with her new husband.

Lake agreed with her plan since he was technically off until next week—he said he didn't plan on going into the office, but he called Zoe to let her know that they were back. He also wanted to fill her in about Dane showing up again and asked her to get him the police reports and send them over. Star loved the way Lake had lived up to his promise of being a team with her and Kai. It was how she saw the three of them now and she was so grateful to have a partner in raising her son. For so long, she felt like she was doing everything by herself—alone against a world of loneliness. But with Lake, she felt like she had finally found where she was supposed to be and who she was supposed to be with.

Lake brought their stuff in from the car and she sat on the edge of the bed, crying. "What's wrong?" Lake asked.

"I never got anything for Kai," she said. "We didn't go into town and I forgot." Lake sat on the bed next to her and pulled her against his body.

"How about this—we tell him that we loved skiing so

much that we've decided to take him back with us and he can pick out his own souvenir?" Lake said.

"You think that will work?" she asked.

"I hope so because I've already booked us a week there over the holidays, in a couple of months. I figured it could be a Christmas surprise. We leave the day after Christmas and we'll be there for the New Year. That work for you?" he asked.

"We'll both have off from school then," she agreed. "Am I going to have to get used to you planning vacations for us and not consulting me first?" she asked.

"Yep," he said, pulling her down onto his body. She snuggled into him, too tired to strip out of her clothes. Lake must have felt the same way because he was softly snoring in no time and she quickly followed him.

Star woke to her cell phone ringing and someone pounding on her front door. "Shit," she grumbled. "What time is it?" She looked at the alarm clock that sat on the bedside table and cursed again. She was going to have to get to the school fast if she wanted to pick Kai up. He probably didn't know that they were back in town unless Gray or Kaiah told him.

"I'm going to be late," she said. "Can you see who's at the door so I can brush my teeth and pull my hair back?" A shower was going to have to wait until later. For now, a change of clothes would be nice and that would give her just enough time to get to the school and pick-up Kai.

"Sure," Lake said. He stood and stretched and Star let her eyes roam his body. So much for spending the day naked and in bed together.

"You keep looking at me like that, Honey, and we won't make it to the school in time to get our boy." Lake pulled on a fresh t-shirt and jeans and ran his hands through his already unruly hair, making her giggle. "I'll get the door and you get ready," he said, giving her a quick kiss.

Star grabbed her toothbrush and followed Lake to the front door. Whoever was on the other side was incisively pounding on it. He pulled it open to find Kaiah and Echo standing on the porch. "What's wrong?" Lake immediately asked.

"I saw something and I'm worried that it's too late. Dane's posted bail," Kaiah said.

"Wait—he has posted bail or you saw it—as in, it hasn't happened yet?" Lake asked.

"He's posted bail," Echo said. "He's out. I confirmed it with the local authorities. He lawyered up and got out."

"Shit," Lake cursed. "Any idea where he is?" he looked at Kaiah knowing that if anyone would have that information, it would be her.

"The school," Kaiah said. "I think he's going after Kai."

"Fuck," Lake shouted, looking back at Star. She ran back to the bathroom and finished brushing her teeth, not bothering to pull her hair back or change, like she wanted to. She had to get to that school before Dane got there. She wouldn't let him take Kai and she was sure that would be his plan.

"Let's go," she ordered. "We have to get to Kai."

"He has proof," Kaiah said. "Your ex has physical proof that you're shifters."

"You want to say that again?" Lake asked. "How did he get proof that we're shifters?"

"He had someone watching you guys, even while you were away. He has video footage of you both in wolf form—Kai, too. I think he's planning on using it against you by involving human hunters," Kaiah said. Star remembered the trouble that Kaiah had with hunters ten years ago when she was with Lake. The last thing any of them needed was human hunters sniffing around, causing trouble.

"Do you have any good news for us?" Lake teased his sister.

Kaiah looked Star over and smiled. "Yeah, but I'll let the two of you figure that part out together." Star wondered what that was all about and grabbed the keys to Lake's truck, pulling him along with her.

"I'm driving," she insisted. "We'll get there faster." Lake looked like he wanted to protest but she got into his truck and started the engine, leaving him no choice but to get into the passenger side of the pick-up. She sped the five miles to the school, hoping that whatever Kaiah saw hadn't happened yet. It would give them a fighting chance if they had a head start on Dane.

They got to the school and Star didn't even bother with finding a parking spot. She double-parked in the bus lane and got out, running for the front entrance to the school. "You go to his classroom and I'll check the dismissal line in the gymnasium," she yelled back over her shoulder to Lake. He nodded and took off in the direction of Kai's classroom and Star said a little prayer that they'd find him.

Star ran into the gym and looked around at the kids who were eager to board buses to go home for the day. She quickly spotted Kaiah's kids and ran over to them. "You guys see Kai?" she asked. She didn't want to upset her new nieces and nephews if Kai wasn't missing but he was usually with them. His not being with them now was sending up red flags for her.

"He left early," one of Kaiah's ten year old's said. They were in the same class with Kai and she figured that they'd know where her son was.

"Left early with who?" Star asked.

Kaiah's son shrugged, "Don't know," he said. "The office called him up during math and said his dad was there to pick him up. Mom told me that Uncle Lake was coming home early and I thought it was him."

"It's all right, Honey," Star soothed. "I'm sure he's fine. You guys get on the bus and go straight home," she ordered.

"Yes, ma'am," they said in unison and she turned to leave the gym. She needed to get to the office and ask who they gave her son to, although she already had a pretty good idea —Dane.

LAKE

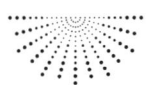

Lake headed into the classroom but didn't find his son. Instead, he found the room empty and the gnawing feeling in the pit of his stomach made him sick. Where was Kai? He hoped that Star had better luck finding him but when he caught up with her at the principal's office, he could tell by the expression on her face that she hadn't.

"Nothing?" she asked

"No," he said. "The room was empty. I'm assuming that you didn't find anything in the gym?"

"Just Kaiah's kids and they told me that Kai was called out of math class saying his dad was here to pick him up," she said. A sob escaped her chest and Lake knew she was about to lose it.

"Shit," he swore. "I can't believe they'd let him go with Dane. Aren't their rules for not letting kids go with strangers?" he asked.

"Technically, Dane isn't a stranger to him. He's still listed on his birth certificate until that paperwork gets updated. The divorce proceedings were easy compared to the custody stuff. That paperwork seems to take a little longer, although I'm sure that the new DNA tests will help. I just can't believe the school secretary would let Kai go with him. She knows that I was away on my honeymoon," Star said.

"Have you ever told anyone about what Dane did to you?" Lake asked.

Star shrugged, "You know it takes me some time to warm up to people. I don't share very much of my personal life with my co-workers, Lake."

"Okay—right now, we need to track down Dane and Kai," Lake said. He was done wasting time when they should be out searching for their son.

Kaiah and Gray found them in the lobby of the school just as they were about to go into the main office. "I know how to track him," Kaiah breathed. "His cell phone."

"I'm not following," Star said.

"We can have his cell phone tracked and that should lead us right to him," Kaiah said.

"That's not a bad idea," Star agreed.

Kaiah smiled up at her husband, "It was Gray's idea."

"Well, don't act so surprised," Gray feigned hurt. "I can have some good ideas sometimes."

"The last time you had one of your famous ideas," Kaiah said. "I ended up pregnant." Gray bobbed his eyes at her and smiled.

"Now, that sounds like a great idea," Gray said.

"Not happening," Kaiah insisted.

"Okay, you two—can we get back to finding my son?" Lake asked. "Remember, he's been abducted. I think we need to call in the local authorities," he said.

"Already done," Gray said.

"You don't have any leads, Sis?" he asked. "You know, using your Jedi mind tricks?"

Kaiah sighed and rolled her eyes, "You watch too many sci-fi shows," she said. "I know that he's safe and he's close. I just can't see where Dane has him."

"I think we need to spread out, cover the reservation, and maybe call in some help. I think if we shift, we'll be able to cover more ground to find him more quickly," Lake said.

"I'll take the kids home and let you know if I see anything," Kaiah said.

"Thanks, Sis," Lake said. He grabbed Star's hand into his own and started for the entrance of the school. "We'll find him, Baby," he promised.

"What if we don't," she asked. He didn't have an answer for her. He'd be lost without their son and Lake knew she felt the same.

"I don't know, Honey," he admitted. "Let's try to stay positive." Star looked across the parking lot, seeming fixated on a black pick-up in the back corner. "What is it?" he asked

"Mom." Lake could hear Kai before he spotted him.

"Kai?" Star called, turning in circles trying to find him. Kai came running across the lot to them and threw his arms around Star's waist.

"You guys came back early," Kai said.

"Where have you been?" Lake asked.

"Dad—well, my other dad said that you told him to pick

DADDY WOLF'S LITTLE STAR

me up. The lady in the office said it was okay because you wrote his name down on my forms," Kai said. Lake couldn't believe that Dane was able to walk out of that school with his son.

"We'll take care of that little hiccup in the morning. I thought you took his name off Kai's forms," Lake asked.

"I did," Star agreed. "Where did Dane take you, Honey?" she asked.

"He took me into town for pizza, and then we went to the park for a little while. Did I do something wrong?" he asked.

"No, Honey," Star lied. "We just didn't know where you were and we were worried. Plus, I was excited to see you again. I missed you," Star said. She looked back to the black pick-up truck that caught her attention earlier.

"What are you thinking, Honey?" Lake whispered into her ear.

Star turned her back to Kai, "I'm thinking that truck looks a lot like the one Dane drove to my house last time I saw him. You think he's taunting me or waiting to talk to me?" she asked.

"Doesn't matter," Lake growled. "You aren't going over to that truck. Take Kai into the school and find my sister and Gray."

"You can't go over there by yourself, Lake," Star protested.

"I can and I will," Lake challenged. "For once, listen to me, Stardust," he ordered.

"Fine but at least wait for Gray," she begged.

Lake nodded, "Tell him to hurry up and meet be over at the truck. Call the cops and tell them to get over here. If it is your ex, I want this over with now." Star nodded and started for the front entrance with Kai. As soon as they were out of sight, Lake walked across the parking lot, dodging school kids as they ran to catch their buses. Lake got to the truck and peeked in to find Dane waiting for him.

"About time," Dane grumbled. "I've been sitting here waiting for you," he said

"Here I am," Lake said, holding his arms wide as if offering himself up to Dane. "What the hell were you doing with my kid? You had no right to take him out of school. He's not your son, Dane. He's not anything to you."

"I raised him. Up until a few months ago, I thought he was my son. You can't take him away from me," Dane challenged.

"I have a DNA test that says otherwise," Lake said.

"DNA?" Dane questioned.

"Yeah—Kai wanted to be tested. He wanted to prove that I'm his father so you'd leave us all alone." Lake knew he was being an ass but he didn't give a fuck. "Why exactly are you here, Dane?" he asked.

"To spend time with Kai and to deliver a little message," he said. "I have proof that you and your tribe here are shifters," Dane said.

"What kind of proof?" Lake asked.

"I have footage of some of you freaks shifting and hunting," Dane said.

"Not sure what you want me to say here, man. I don't give a fuck about your proof," Lake taunted. He was playing it cool but honestly, he was scared to death of what Dane had footage of.

"You might be more interested to know that I'll be

turning over the footage to a group of human hunters," Dane admitted.

"No, you fucking won't?" Lake shouted, garnering a few looks from parents quickly ushering their kids to their cars.

"See, now I've got your attention," Dane said. "I told that bitch that I wanted my revenge and now, I'll have it. Tell Star that I always follow through with my promises." Dane started to put his window up and Lake took a menacing step in his direction, causing him to stop.

"You won't get away with any of this, Dane. You kidnapped my son and I'll be pressing charges. How will that look for your hockey career? You think your adoring fans will hang around when they realize that you've gone batshit crazy and are stalking your ex? You think they'll love you when they hear Star's side of things—how you beat her and verbally abused her for ten years?" Lake knew he wasn't playing fair but the idea of human hunters sniffing around his reservation wasn't one he wanted to entertain.

Dane's smile was mean, "I'm betting we can come to some understanding here, Lake. I mean, that is why you're telling me about you both planning to press charges. How about this—I'll keep my mouth shut and you do the same," Dane offered. Lake hated that the deal Star's ex was offering would mean that he'd get away with kidnapping Kai and terrorizing Star, but he also had a responsibility to his people. Outing the reservation as being home to a pack of wolf shifters was the last thing he needed. It was a trade-off and one that Lake hated having to agree to. He wanted to have Dane tossed in prison and the key thrown away but that would only lead to heartache and trouble for not only his little family but his tribe.

"Fine," Lake spat. "How do I know you won't turn over the footage to the hunters anyway?" he asked.

Dane barked out his laugh, "You don't," he said. "Keep up your end of the bargain and I'll keep up mine," Dane ordered. He put his window up and this time, Lake let him. He needed to get back to Star and Kai and call off the search. Lake stepped away from Dane's pick-up and before he even turned to walk back into the school to look for Star, she was by his side.

"Honey—" Lake started. Star wrapped her arms around his waist.

"I heard," she whispered. "You did the right thing," she said. "He would have exposed us all and that wouldn't be fair to the pack."

"Thank you," Lake said, pulling her against his body. "As chief, I sometimes have to walk a thin line and don't always get to make the easy decisions—you know for my family." Star smiled up at him. "What?" he asked.

"You called us your family," she said. Star shrugged, "It's just nice to hear."

"I've wanted you for so long now, Baby. I'm so damn proud that you and Kai are mine. I know we had a rocky start but I'm thinking we're due some happiness, don't you think?" he asked.

"Yes," she breathed. "Our little family does deserve some happiness."

"How about we get Kai and go on home. We can spend some family time together and then, you and I have a honeymoon to finish," he said. He palmed her ass with his big hands and she gasped.

"Lake, we're in a school parking lot," she whispered.

"No one's around, Honey," he said. "Besides, I've always wanted to make out in the school parking lot like the cool kids," he whispered into her ear. "Let's go home, Mrs. Sani," Lake said.

"I'd go just about anywhere with you, Mr. Sani," Star promised.

EPILOGUE

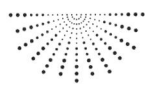

Two months later:

Star shifted back into her human form after a quick run. Lake was right behind her with Kai and she knew she'd only have a few minutes before they got back and she wanted to throw on some clothes and make sure everything was in place for her big surprise.

Just before they left, she came up with some lame excuse about not feeling the best and only going along for part of the shift. She convinced Lake to stay out a little longer with Kai to give them some father/son bonding time. Neither of her guys argued with being able to stay out longer. Kai loved shifting and going for runs with them both, but she knew that her son especially looked forward to his runs with his father. Lake was such a good dad, too. It was fun to watch the relationship blossoming between the two of them.

After everything that happened with her ex, Star worried that they'd struggle in their relationship some. Dane had filled Kai's head with the crazy idea that she was keeping him from seeing her son. He even told Kai that Lake wasn't truly his dad, that Star had lied about the whole thing and when Lake found out what Dane told their son, he just about lost it. But, they sat down, the three of them, and talked about Dane lying to him. Lake even shared the DNA results with Kai and he seemed almost relieved that Dane wasn't being truthful with him.

The next morning, Lake and she had a meeting with the principal and office staff, informing them what happened, and they were assured that Dane had been removed from all of Kai's forms. When Star shared her original restraining order that she had in place from the night Dane had shown up to her house and dislocated her shoulder, they promised that Kai would never be released to her ex again.

As for Dane, they hadn't heard from him since the day he took Kai out of school and that was just fine by her. She just hoped that he kept his side of the bargain because the last thing that her family needed now was trouble from human hunters. If Dane had proof that they were shifters, the whole reservation would be at risk and she'd feel awful about that. As long as he steered clear of them, everything would be fine and one thing she knew for certain about her ex—he loved the fame and fortune that his adoring fans brought him. If he released his proof, Lake would uphold his threat and press charges and she'd be right behind him, adding physical and mental abuse to them. Dane was smart enough to know that Lake meant his promises and she was sure that his career was more important to him than the revenge he promised her he'd have. At least, she hoped that was the case.

She pulled her clothes on, that she tossed onto the porch when they stripped for their shift and went into their little cabin. Kaiah had been by with a few of Star's teacher friends from the school to decorate their place. She was going to tell Lake and Kai that she was pregnant and what better way to do it than with balloons and a cake. Kaiah had taken care of everything and she was so thankful.

"There you are," Kaiah said from the kitchen. Her sister-in-law put her hands on her hips and smiled. "You're cutting it a little close for the big reveal. You ready?" She had to admit, she was a little nervous to tell Lake that she was pregnant. Of course, Kaiah had known for months but didn't tell her. Things were so crazy from their quicky marriage to everything that went down with her ex, she didn't even realize that she was pregnant until she missed her third period.

"I'm a little nervous," she whispered. Kaiah pulled her in for a quick hug.

"You'll be great," she said. "My brother is going to be thrilled to be a dad again and Kai will be such an awesome big brother. My crew will be here in a few minutes, so it's about to get pretty crazy in here. You've got this," Kaiah assured.

Star nodded, "I'm going to run back to the bathroom and freshen up, and then I'll come out to help with any last-minute touches," she said.

"Sounds good," Kaiah said. Star disappeared back into the master bedroom and rummaged through her closet, looking for the gift she got for Lake. She wanted to give him something to commemorate him being a dad. It might not be their first child together, but it was the first one that Lake would be around for from the beginning, and she hoped to make it a big deal. She had gotten him a key chain that said, "#1 Dad" with Kai's picture on the front. Star ran a brush through her long, dark hair and powdered her nose before hearing the ruckus of Kaiah's kids in the family room. She giggled to herself at how noisy her brood was. By the time she got back down to the family room, half of Kaiah's kids were trying to stick their fingers in the cake and the other half were playing wrestle mania in the middle of the room. Star couldn't help her smile thinking that someday, this might be her life. She wanted lots of kids and she knew that Lake did too. She was an only child and Lake had grown up as one, not meeting his half-sisters until he was an adult. They wanted a whole houseful of kids together.

"Sorry," Kaiah said, looking at her boys wrestling in the family room. "Gray was supposed to keep them in check but Lake and Kai got back early from their run and he's stalling them on the porch. You ready?"

"No one else is here," Star said.

"I know but they can just join in on the fun once they get here. Dad's on his way. It's now or never, Star. I'm betting that my hooligans will topple the cake and eat it off the floor if you don't let Lake in and give him your news." Star giggled and nodded.

"Let's do this then," she agreed. She met Lake and Kai at the door and opened it to reveal the houseful of chaos, filled with pink and blue balloons.

"What's all this?" Lake asked. Kaiah stood in the corner of the room smiling at him and Lake shot a look over his shoulder at Gray. "Are congratulations in order, man?" he asked Gray. "You finally talk my sister into kid number nine or maybe even ten?" he teased.

Gray slapped Lake on the back and laughed, "Congratulations are in order, brother, but not for me." Star watched Lake, waiting for him to catch up.

"Wait—this is for us?" he asked. Star couldn't help her tears—stupid hormones, as she nodded and threw herself into his arms.

"Yes," she whispered. "I'm pregnant," she said.

"Pregnant, as in we're having a baby?" Lake asked.

"Yep," Kaiah said, pulling her brother in for a quick hug as soon as Star released him. "That's what pregnant means," she teased.

"How long have you known?" Lake asked Star. She was beginning to worry that he wasn't as happy about the baby as she hoped he would be.

"Just about a week. I'm about three months pregnant," she said. "With everything that happened, I guess I just missed the signs."

"I knew," Kaiah boasted.

"And, you didn't tell either of us?" Lake asked.

"Not my place," she said. "Besides, this is a lot more fun. I don't think I've ever seen you so tongue-tied and twisted up, Lake."

"Am not," he countered. "I'm just surprised."

"Good surprised?" Star asked. She felt as if she was holding her breath waiting for his answer.

"Yes," he promised. "Good surprised." Lake pulled her back up against his body to gently kiss her lips and she felt all the stress leave her body—he was happy about the baby and that was all she needed to hear.

"How about you, Kai," Gray asked. "You happy to have a little brother or sister?"

Kai eagerly nodded his head, making them all laugh. "Yes," he agreed. "But, I hope it's a boy," he said. "Girls are yucky," he said, wrinkling up his nose. Kaiah's girls protested and pulled Lake into the family room's wrestling arena.

"You want a girl or a boy?" Lake asked.

"Doesn't matter," Star admitted. "How about you?"

"Same, but I'd love a little girl who looks just like her mama," Lake whispered into her ear. "Love you."

"I love you too, Lake," she said.

The rest of their friends and family showed up and they all celebrated their little one and Star wasn't sure how she had gotten so lucky. Lake had been the man she had always wanted. He was her second chance at happiness and she'd forever be grateful that he gave her that. She had finally found a life with the man she had always loved—her first love, her forever, her Northern star, her home.

The End

I hope you enjoyed Lake and Star's story. Now, buckle up for your inside sneak peek at Daddy Wolf's Little Heartbreaker (Silver Wolf Shifters Book 4).

WILLOW

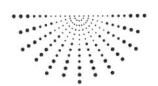

"He's here again," Roger growled. "That guy that comes in here and gawks at you for hours, drinks a total of two beers, leaves my girls shitty tips, and then takes off." Willow rolled her eyes at her boss. Roger owned one of the many strip clubs that dotted the seedier back alleys in New Orleans. People who frequented streets like the ones where her club was located were either looking for a psychic reading, a warm willing woman, or strippers who promised to tease and please. Willow was the latter and she had to admit, the money was shit but Roger made the clientele keep their fucking hands to themselves and that was her favorite part.

"What do you want me to do about it, Rodger?" she asked. Honestly, she didn't mind the guy. He kept to himself and didn't try to talk to her after she was done on stage. Hell, he didn't even stick around after she finished her routine and that was just fine by her.

"I don't know," Rodger mumbled. "Just do your fucking job and put on a good show. This place needs a boost and if you can't do that for me then I'll hire some young, hot piece of ass that can." He started out of the dressing room and stopped dead when she "Yeah, yeah, yeahed," him but Rodger was too much of a pussy to turn around and challenge her. Most men were afraid of her and Willow decided a long time ago that she was fine with that. Ten years ago, to be exact. That was when her whole life changed. It was when her older sister and she were abducted by wolf shifters and held captive. The wolves took her innocence because her sister double-crossed them. Lilith had left to find happiness and Willow was the one who paid the price for her sister's disobedience. She was still paying the price because she'd never been able to escape the feel of them taking her body against her will, the stench of their breath on her skin, the dirty, disgusting things they whispered into her ear. No, they were a part of her now—it was who she was and one lonely guy sitting at the end of the bar watching her was the least of her problems.

"One of these days," Rodger growled, "someone's going to knock you in that pretty, smart ass mouth of yours, Willow." He didn't wait around for her to give a sassy remark this time, quickly walking out of the dimly lit back room.

WILLOW GOT up to the stage just as soon as she heard the bass from her song thumping through the ancient sound system. "Good luck," the new girl whispered to her, and

Willow rolled her eyes. She hated the new girl and that's probably why she didn't even take the time to learn her name. Nope—she was forever going to be the new girl.

"Thanks, New Girl," Willow said and she even went the extra mile to pat the young woman on the top of her head, like someone would a new puppy. Yeah, it was a dick move, but she didn't give a fuck.

Willow stepped out onto the stage and got a few catcalls from some of the regulars. Things were slow again tonight and she was beginning to wonder if it was time to move on—find another club, maybe even a younger crowd. But, at thirty-one, not many clubs like that would welcome her. There was the other option, one that she had been thinking about for some time now but deep down, she knew it might land her back into the same hot water she found herself in when the Devils abducted her and her sister. She had heard of special clubs in town—ones that catered to shifters. They only hired shifter dancers and as a fox shifter, she'd fit the bill. The only problem was going to be hiding her gift and keeping her ass out of trouble. Willow was a seer too and that was the part of herself that she had to keep carefully hidden. It was what the Devils wanted, what most packs in the area were hunting down—shifters with special abilities.

Willow followed her routine, not having to work up too much of a sweat. She knew the damn thing by heart—swing around the pole at the chorus, drop it like it's hot, and then slide back up the pole, staring out into the audience seductively, to make each member in the dark room believe she's looking directly at him. Yeah, she had the routine down cold and God, she was ready for a change. But that would mean trusting her instincts again and taking a leap of faith to venture out into the world. None of those things appealed to her anymore. She was more of a "play it safe" kind of girl now and who could blame her for wanting to keep things that way? At thirty-one, she had lived more life than most women had by fifty. She suffered heartache, betrayal, pain, and suffering, and still found her way forward through it all to make a life for herself. Sure, it was a shitty life, but it was hers.

Willow finished up her routine to a less than rousing round of applause and she quickly took her bow, gathering up the few dollars that had been thrown onto the stage. She bent down to retrieve a twenty from the stage and for just a split second, Willow wondered if her luck had changed. She should have known better, really. As she picked up the twenty, the guy who had been there night after night gawking at her, the cheep one who only drank two beers and tipped for shit—he chose tonight to make his move. He just about climbed onto the stage and grabbed her arm. Willow shouted for Rodger but he was across the club behind the bar. He had foolishly let all his bouncers go, saying that he couldn't afford to pay them anymore, and even went as far as blaming the women dancing in the club for that. He told them that if they were any good, they'd need a bouncer's protection but since they were shit, he felt confident enough to get rid of the guys he had originally hired to protect them. Guys she could use about now to help remove this asshole from the stage and help release the death grip he had on her arm.

"Miss me, Willow?" he growled in her ear, pinning her to

the sticky stage, almost climbing on top of her. She panicked and thrashed around but it did her no good. The guy was at least three times bigger than her and seemed pretty intent on reminding her who he was—not that she'd ever forgotten him.

"Boomer," she whispered. He was the guy in charge over at the Devils. The one who had eluded the authorities all this time. He was the one causing her to watch over her shoulder every time the hair on the back of her neck stood on end and she just felt like something was off. Boomer was the man that nightmares were made of. He raped her, taking her virginity and when he was finished with her, he passed her onto the next member in the Devils standing in line for his turn. How did she not recognize him before? He looked different now—older and his once blond hair was now almost jet black, but it was him. She'd remember the stench of day-old booze and cigarettes for the rest of her life.

"Yeah—I think you did," he growled. "It's been a long time, little fox," he said.

"I—I didn't tell them who you were. Not ever," she swore. She had pretended to help Colt Sutton out with his case. He was FBI and when she figured out that Sutton was one of the two shifters with her sister, she told him she didn't know anything else, and eventually, she took off and stopped helping him. Willow was smart enough to know that telling anyone who Boomer was would end badly for her, so she never did.

"Doesn't matter, Honey," he breathed into her hair. "You've been a hard one to track down but you and your sister are the last two loose ends in my little puzzle. I'm betting you can help me find Lilith and then the three of us can have a little party." The thought of him touching her again made her sick to her stomach. Every time he forcefully took her body, he told her that they were going to "have a little party" and she'd immediately be able to taste the stomach bile in her mouth.

"I—I don't know where Lilith is," she admitted. It was the truth. She hadn't had any contact with her sister in ten years. Colt had been her only lifeline to Lilith and when she found out who he was, she immediately cut him out. The last thing she wanted was to have a connection with her older sister. She was the reason that Boomer did what he had to her. All Lilith had to do was return for her and none of the ugly, gut-wrenching shit she went through would have happened.

Boomer chuckled in her ear, "Now see," he whispered. "I don't believe you, Willow." She heard him grunt and then he collapsed on top of her.

"You okay, Willow?" a woman's small voice asked.

"New Girl?" Willow questioned. New Girl rolled Boomer off her and onto the dirty dance floor.

"Yeah," she said. "Rodger said he warned you and that you were probably getting what your smart mouth deserved. So, I grabbed the baseball bat he keeps behind the bar, and well, I think I might have killed this guy." Willow wanted to laugh at the way New Girl was gingerly poking Boomer with the baseball bat.

"One can only hope," Willow grumbled. "But, I'm pretty sure he's still breathing." New Girl stopped poking Boomer long enough to reach a hand down to Willow to help her up.

"You okay?" she asked.

"No," she admitted. "But, I will be. I need to get out of here," Willow said. "Thanks for the help." New Girl nodded and smiled, playfully resting the bat on her shoulder.

"Anytime," she said. "Be safe, Willow."

"You too," Willow said. She grabbed the bat from New Girl and rushed off the stage to the back dressing room. "Slugger," she said back over her shoulder, not missing the way New Girl smiled at her new nickname. With any luck, she'd have enough time to get her shit cleared out of her locker and high tail it back to her apartment to pack her stuff. If Boomer found her at the club, he'd probably know where she lived, and letting him make good on his promises wasn't something she was willing to wait around for.

CAMERON

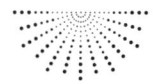

Cameron Jackson watched as Willow Mercury took off through the back of the club into the dark alleyway. He had been undercover with the Devils for so long now that he had heard all the nasty rumors about the sexy little fox who was nervously checking over her shoulder. It was time to call this into his boss and figure out what to do next. Blowing his cover wasn't something he was willing to do but hurting Willow was against his direct orders from his upper ups.

"Sutton," his boss barked into the cell.

"Hey Colt," Cam said trying for casual, though he felt anything but.

"What do you have for me, man?" Colt asked, cutting right to the chase.

"Willow," Cam breathed. "You were right, Boomer was on her trail and he's found her."

"Fuck," Colt swore into the other end of the call. He

followed it up with an impressive string of curses that would make a sailor blush. "How the hell did he find her and we couldn't?"

"Don't know boss, but he has," Cameron said.

"Where is he taking her?" Colt asked.

"He doesn't have her," Cam admitted. "He went into the club about an hour ago and told me to wait in the car, just like every other night he's been here. He's usually out sooner than this and I was about to go in after him but then I saw Willow leaving through the back alley, behind the building. I'm betting things didn't go too well for Boomer or he'd have her by now. At least, that's my guess. What do you want me to do?" Cameron asked.

Colt sighed into the other end of the cell. "This is fucked up. If I have you go after her, you could blow your cover with Boomer and we've worked too damn hard to get you in good with him and the Devils. But, I can't lose Willow again—it's been ten years."

"So, go after her then?" Cameron confirmed, trying to follow Colt's ramblings.

"Fuck," he shouted. "Yes—go after her and once you get her, don't let her go."

"Will do, boss," Cam agreed.

"Take her to the safe house and wait for further instructions," Colt ordered. "I'll be in touch." Colt ended the call and Cam started the car. Willow had taken off for the bus stop and if he didn't find her before one of Boomer's other guys, she wasn't going to make it onto the bus. She was being careless and Cam worried that he was already too late.

He pulled over a few blocks down from the bus stop and

parked the car. He was glad that the stop was on the dark street corner. He'd hopefully be able to slip in, drug Willow and then get her back to his car, without attracting too much notice. Cameron hid in the shadows, making his way over to the bus enclosure only to find it empty.

"Shit," he whispered to himself. The little fox had given him the slip. "She was just here a few seconds ago," he grumbled.

"Still here asshole," a woman's voice growled from behind him. He swung around to find her half-naked and her curvy, sexy body was enough of a distraction that he let his guard down—just for a minute, but that was long enough for Willow's baseball bat to meet the side of his skull. A searing pain shot through his head and he fell to the ground, his knees hitting the pavement with a thud. The pain was too much and Cam knew he was going to pass out, leaving him at Willow's mercy and right about now, the woman didn't look very merciful. She stood over his body tapping the baseball bat to her hand as if letting him know that getting up would be a bad idea. Yeah—he got it. He'd stay down and not give her another reason to hit him again.

"Let's talk, asshole," Willow said. He hated to tell her but Cam's ability to hold a conversation was about to get a whole lot more difficult given the fact that he wasn't going to be conscious. "Shit—" Willow knelt to the ground next to him and he tried to reach for her, pull her in closer, and warn her. "Don't you fucking pass out on me," she ordered. His hand swiped uncontrollably through the air and she jumped back, just out of reach.

"Willow," he mumbled.

"You don't get to say my name, asshole," she spat, leaning back over his body. He gave up trying to grab her but he needed to warn her. Cameron had a feeling that Boomer met Willow's bat and if that was the case, he wouldn't stay down long. His wolf would heal him and he'd come after her. Boomer was ruthless and there would be nothing that Cam could do to protect her if the Devils' Prez came looking for her now, at least not until his wolf healed him. Cam needed to tell her to go—to run, but his mouth wasn't forming words.

"Danger," he choked.

"Yeah," Willow sneered. "I bet you are. Guess you assholes didn't plan on me having this," she said, palming the bat. "Or the fact that a little fox shifter could be badass enough to take on a couple of wolves. I vowed I'd never let another one of you Devils lay a finger on me," she said.

"He's coming," Cameron insisted. With each passing second, his body was healing itself. His head was feeling a little less fuzzy and he worried that Boomer was experiencing the same. "Boomer will find you," he warned.

"Oh—I don't know," she sassed. "I'm betting that you're pretty important to old Bom. Maybe I should take you and hold you in a cage just like you fuckers did me," she threatened. Willow stood and held the bat to his head. "You gonna come willingly or am I going to have to knock you out and drag your body back to your car?" she asked.

Cameron tried to sit up, groaning, and holding his head. "Willingly," he croaked. Willow made no move to help him from the pavement, standing back, wearily watching his every move. He knew she had the goods to knock him on his ass again and he'd do just about anything to avoid another blow to his head with her baseball bat. The woman had damn good aim and an incredible arm. If he could get to his feet, he'd let her believe she was in charge and the one taking him. Hell, he'd let her believe just about anything she'd like if it meant he'd be able to get her the fuck off the street corner and someplace safe. He was sure that Boomer finding them would end badly for one or both of them. There was no way he wanted to blow his cover and putting Colt Sutton's sister-in-law in danger again wasn't an option. He was pretty sure that his boss would not only have his badge, but he'd also kick his ass into next week if Boomer got his hands on Willow again.

"Keys," she spat, holding out her hand. He pulled them from his pocket and tossed them to her. She led him over to the sedan that he drove for Boomer. They'd have to ditch the car at some point and lay low but first, he was going to have to convince the sexy little fox shifter that he was on her side and from the angry scowl on her beautiful face, he was going to have a whole lot of convincing to do.

Willow popped the trunk and poked him in the back with the bat. "Get in, fucker," she ordered.

He panicked at the idea of being locked in the small, dark space. "In the trunk?" he stuttered.

"Yep," she quickly agreed. "You're new home away from home until I can find another cage to stick your ass in," she said. She shoved the bat into his back again, this time using just a little more force. "We can do this the hard way and I pop your kneecaps from behind, forcing you into the trunk or you climb your ass in on your own. How's this gonna go down?" she asked. God, she sounded almost happy about inflicting pain on him and he was pretty sure she'd do it. "With or without pain—it's your call."

Cameron sighed and carefully climbed into the trunk, breathing through the anxiety that riddled the pit of his core. He peeked out at her had held up his hands, as if trying to stop her from shutting the truck in his face. "Before you do this, Willow," he whispered. "I just want you to know that I'm on your side."

Her laugh rang out through the night and he knew that there was nothing he could say to make her believe him. "I'm sure you are, asshole," she spat and lowered the truck, slamming it shut, leaving him in total darkness.

"That went well," he breathed.

DADDY WOLF'S Little Heartbreaker (Silver Wolf Shifters Book 4) coming soon!

ABOUT K.L. RAMSEY & BE KELLY

Romance Rebel fighting for
Happily Ever After!

K. L. Ramsey currently resides in West Virginia (Go Mountaineers!). In her spare time, she likes to read romance novels, go to WVU football games and attend book club (aka-drink wine) with girlfriends. K. L. enjoys writing Contemporary Romance, Erotic Romance, and Sexy Ménage! She loves to write strong, capable women and bossy, hot as hell alphas, who fall ass over tea kettle for them. And of course, her stories always have a happy ending. But wait—there's more!

Somewhere along the writing path, K.L. developed a love of ALL things paranormal (but has a special affinity for shifters <YUM!!>)!! She decided to take a chance and create another persona- BE Kelly- to bring you all of her yummy shifters, seers, and everything paranormal (plus a hefty dash of MC!).

K. L. RAMSEY'S SOCIAL MEDIA

Ramsey's Rebels - K.L. Ramsey's Readers Group
https://www.facebook.com/groups/ramseysrebels

KL Ramsey & BE Kelly's ARC Team
https://www.facebook.com/groups/klramseyandbekellyarcteam

KL Ramsey and BE Kelly's Newsletter
https://mailchi.mp/4e73ed1b04b9/authorklramsey/

KL Ramsey and BE Kelly's Website
https://www.klramsey.com

facebook.com/kl.ramsey.58
instagram.com/itsprivate2
bookbub.com/profile/k-l-ramsey
twitter.com/KLRamsey5

BE KELLY'S SOCIAL MEDIA

BE Kelly's Reader's group
https://www.facebook.com/groups/kellsangelsreadersgroup/

- facebook.com/be.kelly.564
- instagram.com/bekellyparanormalromanceauthor
- twitter.com/BEKelly9
- bookbub.com/profile/be-kelly

WORKS BY K. L. RAMSEY

The Relinquished Series Boxed Set

Love Times Infinity

Love's Patient Journey

Love's Design

Love's Promise

Harvest Ridge Series Box Set

Worth the Wait

The Christmas Wedding

Line of Fire

Torn Devotion

Fighting for Justice

Last First Kiss Series Box Set

Theirs to Keep

Theirs to Love

Theirs to Have

Theirs to Take

Second Chance Summer Series

True North

The Wrong Mister Right

Ties That Bind Series

Saving Valentine

Blurred Lines

Dirty Little Secrets

Taken Series

Double Bossed

Double Crossed

Double The Mistletoe

Owned

His Secret Submissive

His Reluctant Submissive

His Cougar Submissive

His Nerdy Submissive (Coming soon)

Alphas in Uniform

Hellfire

His Destiny (Coming soon)

Royal Bastards MC

Savage Heat

Whiskey Tango

Savage Hell MC Series

Roadkill

REPOssession

Dirty Ryder

Girl Power Romance Series/Scarlet Letter Series

Hard Limits

No Limits (Coming soon)

Dirty Desire Series

Torrid (Coming soon)

Smokey Bandits MC Series

Aces Wild (Coming soon)

Mountain Men Mercenary Series (Coming soon)

Deadly Sins Syndicate (Mafia Series) (Coming soon)

Pride

Envy

Greed

Lust

Wrath

Sloth

Gluttony

WORKS BY BE KELLY (K.L.'S ALTER EGO...)

Reckoning MC Seer Series

Reaper

Tank

Raven

Perdition MC Shifter Series

Ringer

Rios

Trace

Wren's Pack (Coming soon)

Silver Wolf Shifter Series

Daddy Wolf's Little Seer

Daddy Wolf's Little Captive

Daddy Wolf's Little Star

Demonic Retribution Series

Sinner (Coming soon)

Graystone Academy Series (Coming soon)

Made in the USA
Columbia, SC
25 August 2023